Robot Empire: Dawn Exodus

Robot Empire, Volume 1

Kevin Partner

Published by Trantor Press, 2017.

This is a work of fiction. Similarities to real people, places, or events are entirely coincidental.

ROBOT EMPIRE: DAWN EXODUS

First edition. October 16, 2017.

Written by Kevin Partner.

To my dad, Doug, who always encouraged my love of science

Flight

DATE: FIRST CONTACT minus 22.5 hours.

They'd been chasing him for days, like a wolf pack on the scent, relentlessly narrowing the distance between his ship and theirs. It was only a matter of time before they caught him and there was only one penalty for attempting to escape from the colonies of the Vanis Federation. Especially with what he had in the cargo hold.

Hal threw the chart down and ran his hands over his face. He'd planned to make for the belt of asteroids that circled between the fifth and sixth planets of the Vanis system but a blip on the ladar had warned him, in the nick of time, that an interceptor waited there. It was as if they'd known what he was planning all along. Or perhaps they simply assumed that someone would make a break for it and so had placed their ships on the periphery.

It was no good thinking about it too much. He very much doubted they'd anticipated anyone would steal what he had stored feet away from him, glowing feebly in the darkness. And yet what use would it be to him if he couldn't escape, couldn't find anyone willing to pay what it was worth? He'd never make it to the gate and a random jump through interstellar space; if his ion drive couldn't keep him ahead of them until he found somewhere to hide, he was lost.

"This is the destroyer Relentless, hailing the..." the voice paused for a moment, "...unclassified vessel. You are ordered to disengage your ion drive and prepare to be boarded."

Hal bit back his annoyance at the arrogance and disdain in the voice, but he couldn't quite stop himself responding. "This is the launch Knox. Don't waste your breath."

"Knox, your situation is already serious, I suggest you do not make it fatal. Pull over and return what you have stolen."

Hal wasn't a fool. He knew that he'd signed his death warrant the moment he'd stepped on board the Knox and engaged its drive without an official flight plan. That would have been bad enough, but he'd carried something more valuable than the colony itself in an old canvas bag that now sat in the hold. Stealing that would have ensured the slow death of himself and his family. But the Vanis had seen to it that he had no family, so the only neck on the line was his own.

The NavSkem showed the Vanis craft trailing the Knox. At the bottom of the display, the separation distance was being counted down like an executioner's pocket watch - when it reached zero he'd be dead. "Nav, how soon to intercept?"

Assuming no deviation in velocity by either craft, intercept in four hours, fourteen minutes and 10 seconds.

Leaning back as the metallic voice of the nav computer died away, Hal sighed. "And are there any debris fields, asteroids or anywhere else I can reach in less than four hours?"

Sorry, I don't understand the question. Please rephrase it in such a way that I can perform the required calculation.

Hal grunted. He'd known the stupid thing would respond like that, after all it wasn't an AI. How could it be? AIs no longer existed.

Sensors detect weapons discharge from the pursuing ship.

That got his attention. "What sort of weapons?"

High-intensity laser.

"Time to impact?"

2 minutes.

What were they playing at? Lasers were fearsome weapons at close quarters, but they travelled in a straight line, so avoiding a laser with two minutes warning was like dodging a very small glacier.

"Evasive manoeuvres." He guessed they were just trying to frighten him, trying to make a show of their power.

Command not understood. What do you wish to evade?

Hal jumped to his feet and banged his fist on the console. "The laser, for frak's sake!"

The laser is not aimed at this vessel, I cannot, therefore, program a course to evade it.

"What is it aimed at, then?"

Calculating...

Hal glanced back at the NavSkem. It showed his ship, the pursuing vessels and any bodies massive enough to affect navigation.

Calculating...

The problem was that there were thousands of moving objects within a radius of a hundred kilometres of the ship and the NavCom was working out the positions of each of them relative to the incoming laser.

Calculating...

"Limit candidates to objects above 100 tonnes mass." That did it.

Calculated.

A red blob appeared on the NavSkem.

"They're targeting a meteoroid. Emergency course correction, take us away from the targeted object, maximum possible negative velocity."

Acknowledged.

Hal grabbed the console as the ship lurched to the side, he leaned sideways, then corrected himself as his ride smoothed out.

"Activate rear viewer."

The NavSkem disappeared and a 3D view of the space behind the ship grew out of the console surface. It was hard to tell, at first, that they were moving at all, but then he began to notice tiny objects flashing backwards. These were the debris and meteoroids of the Vanis System set against the unmoving backdrop of the stars. Then, as he watched, a section of the view exploded then immediately faded again. He didn't need to ask the NavCom how close that had been to the ship's previous position. The Vanis had used the computer against him - they'd known it could evade a laser aimed directly at him, so they'd blown up a lump of rock nearby that the NavCom would ignore. And if he'd continued on his previous course he'd have had a face full of asteroid. It wouldn't have destroyed his ship, but it would probably have disabled it. Exactly as intended.

It really came to something, didn't it, when his was the smartest brain on the ship? Oh, the NavCom could beat him in a calculating contest every time and with one transistor tied behind its back. But give it a simple problem that required judgement and intuition and it was nothing more than a glorified adding machine. This all meant that it was his brain against the combined intelligence of all the officers on the Relentless - and they couldn't all be idiots.

"Activate NavSkem," he said and watched as the holographic view of surrounding space rebuilt itself. The last object to be added was the chasing ship. It looked a lot closer.

"Calculate time to intercept."

At current velocity and vector, Relentless will overtake us in 2 hours 35 minutes and 33 seconds.

"Damn it!"

Hal began pacing up and down the tiny compartment that served as the bridge of the Knox. He felt like a dog in a corporation kennel, hoping for its owner to arrive but knowing, in its heart, that it was doomed. So, Relentless had anticipated his move when they'd targeted the lump of rock. In truth they'd probably expected him to be disabled, but veered on their current course just in case the pilot they were chasing saw through their tactic. He felt a moment of pride as he realised that he had, at least, forced them to plan B.

But it would only delay the inevitable. What he needed was an advantage. Knox was more manoeuvrable than Relentless, but couldn't compete in sheer speed. Knox was also more or less weaponless so any direct encounter would only end one way. The only other thing he had on board that the Relentless didn't was the glowing cube in his hold.

He moved to the back of the bridge and pulled down the lock on the cargo bay door before stepping through into what was not so much a hold as a glorified cupboard. There sat the canvas bag, a red pulsing visible through the many tears in the fabric. Hal pulled apart the handles and undid the zip. There it was, the most valuable object in the Vanis Federation. Had he not timed things so perfectly, he'd now have their entire fleet on his back, but Relentless had been the only ship in the area when he'd made his escape.

Hal reached in and pulled out a cube, each side approximately the length of his index fingers. It lay in his hands beating like an artificial heart. What did it contain to make the Vanis protect it so carefully? Data? Star maps of lost systems? It was clearly of huge value and only by a combination of good luck and long preparation had Hal got close to it, and he was even luckier to get away. He wondered whether, at last, his luck had run out.

"What are you?" he said as he turned the object over and over in his hands.

It made no response but continued to pulse in a slow rhythm.

Hal lowered the cube back into the bag. "Pity, I could do with a hand escaping the Vanis."

You wish to escape the Vanis Federation?

Hal dropped the cube and fell backwards. It lay in his bag, the slow pulsing replaced by a frantically cycling colourscape.

Hal Chen, you wish to escape the Vanis Federation? The female voice said from across the small room.

Scrambling onto his knees, Hal crawled across the floor and peered into the bag where the cube sat kaleidoscopically.

"Yes, I have..." he paused to find the right word, "...rescued you, and now the Vanis are pursuing me, they will intercept within two hours. By the gods, are you an AI?"

I am ACE. I have accessed your NavCom. Your current course will result in my recapture, I am therefore plotting alternative vectors. Please wait.

Hal reached in and picked the cube up again. It felt warm to the touch as if it were alive again after many years in hibernation. "I thought all the AIs had gone, more than a century ago."

I am currently processing multiple vectors. Formal introductions will have to wait. Please give me access to your guidance system and sensing array - your star maps are out of date.

"How do I give you access?"

Command your NavCom. It is currently being rather rigid in its interpretation of security and access protocols.

Hal leaned back into the doorway to the bridge. "NavCom, grant all access to the entity known as ACE."

Acknowledged

"Do you have the access you need?"

Affirmative. Processing. Interesting. Your sensing array records the position of a large object that is not included in the star charts.

"How does that help?"

It is likely that the pursuing ship uses the same star maps as your vessel. They may not be aware of the object. It is a nickel-iron asteroid of considerable mass. It is likely that we could find a ravine or fissure in which to hide. To the pursuing ship, we will seem to have vanished.

Hal had, by this time, returned to the canvas bag and had pulled the cube out. It seemed oddly rude to talk to ACE while she was at the bottom of a dirty old rucksack. She? Yes, it was hard not to see ACE as a person. He'd never made that mistake with NavCom or any other computer system, but ACE felt real and alive in a way he'd never experienced before. Maybe the Archaists had a point, he could see how people could come to rely on the help of AIs a little too much. But this particular beggar couldn't afford to be a chooser.

"Can we make it to the asteroid before they catch us?"

Success is within the tolerances of my best estimate.

"You mean you don't know?" Hal said, looking down at the cube which seemed to be sporting less exuberant colours. "What can we do to increase our chances?"

This ship has primitive automated systems. It responds best when piloted manually so that last minute adjustments can be made.

"You want me to fly the ship?"

The globe exploded into light and sudden unbearable heat. Hal threw it away and it rolled into a corner, all colour had vanished along with any sign of intelligence.

No, I want ***us*** *to fly it.*

Hal threw his hands over his ears. The voice seemed to be coming from inside his head. "Where are you?"

When you picked me up, I detected your cranial implants. They are of inefficient design, but they will serve. Now, we will fly the ship together. Do exactly as I say and we might survive.

Hal staggered onto the bridge and sat in the tall command chair, his hand still on his temple. He felt as though madness had been injected directly into his brain.

"Will you leave my implant when we escape?" he said out loud.

First we must escape.

The Choosing

DATE: FIRST CONTACT minus 5 years

As the light faded and dusk approached, Arla lay on her back and looked through the sky to the fields beyond. This was her favourite thing to do, all the more so because it was a rarity. It needed both a dry, cloudless, atmosphere and the opportunity for her to slip away for a few hours, and that sort of combination only came up once in a while.

There had been no rain for several days and none was expected that evening, so she'd been on the lookout for an opportunity to lose herself amongst all the bustle of the preparations for the ceremony tomorrow. She'd been desperate for one last look because, even though she believed it vanishingly unlikely that she'd be selected, the ceremony marked the passage to true adulthood for all those that attended. A new and privileged life awaited the selected few, though with no prospect of a family of their own; no husband or children, no father or mother. But for the majority who stayed behind, it was time for responsibility and marriage, so a different sort of selection awaited them. A selection she planned to put off for as long as possible: fifteen felt like far too young to be making choices that would affect the rest of her life.

Arla's gaze swept the sky as she pushed thoughts of matchmaking, long years of labour in the fields and the horrific thought of childbirth out of her mind. This view would last only a couple of minutes and this might well be the final time she'd see it. There. A light twinkled in the heavens or, more correctly, on the other side of them. As the sun faded, she was looking at the other side of the world. Perhaps the light was from a bonfire lit to celebrate the forthcoming ceremonies which took place all over the world on midsummer night. As her eyes adjusted to the gathering gloom, other twinkles appeared and she imagined young people and old joining hands as they danced around them. She half expected to hear their voices carrying across the emptiness.

Arla could see lights in two broad bands that ran either side of the sun, which was now completely extinguished but remained as an invisible barrier blocking her view of any celebratory bonfires behind it.

She lay there as the night breeze played across her face. She felt at one with the world, as if she and it were a single entity, at total peace with one another.

"Mistress, I must ask you to return to the farm."

Arla sighed. She wasn't surprised. She'd known that R.DJ would be the first to notice her absence. He would look for her and, when he didn't find her, he'd go to his master, her father, and report that she was missing. And her father would growl at him to get his metal hide up the mountain and bring her back.

It wasn't Deejay's fault. He was a robot and bound to obey his master by laws as inviolate as those that governed human behaviour. Robots were the uncomplaining servants sent by the blessed Engineers to aid the people toiling in the fields. Just as

God had humans to do her bidding, so those humans had machines to serve them.

"Mistress, we must make haste. Curfew begins in 61 minutes."

Arla looked up at the robot. He loomed over her, his artificial eyes glowing a faint yellow that flickered gently as he waited for her response. His exoskeleton was of plastic and aluminium, though pitted and dented with the little accidents that had accumulated over the centuries, and he weighed several times as much as she did. He could snap her in two without effort, and yet she had no fear as he stood there, patiently waiting. This was partly the simple familiarity that came from growing up with these eager-to-please servants always on the periphery of her vision. But it was also because she knew that there was one law that robots considered even more sacrosanct than the one that compelled them to obey orders - it was that they must not, under any circumstances, harm a human or allow a human to come to harm. This was a fact as certain and inviolate as the earth beneath her back and the cylindrical sun above her head.

She watched the tell-tale flicker in his eyes that suggested he was coming to a decision. He had been given an order to fetch her, but she had failed, so far, to comply despite his repeated request. By not responding, she had given him an implied order to wait. But now the direct command of his master was overriding his hesitation and he was about to speak.

Arla decided to put him out of his misery. She took a final look up at the sky which was now fully dark. As always, the lights had disappeared, though she suspected they were still there. It was as if some sort of invisible barrier had been extended between the two hemispheres.

"Will you carry me, Deejay?"

The flicker went from the robot's eyes and she felt momentarily guilty that she'd stressed him. But, after all, he wasn't human, so he didn't have feelings. "Certainly mistress," Deejay said and, bending down, he slid his arms under her with infinite care and lifted her to his chest. He turned with a grace that was only marred by the slight squeaking of his axis joint and carried her down the mountain.

"Where have you been?" roared her father when she appeared at the door, half asleep in the arms of R.DJ.

"You know where she's been, Jabe, she's been up on the mountain where she has no right goin'." A woman wearing a poisoned expression shuffled in from the kitchen door, waving a wooden spoon as if dispensing justice.

Fully awake now, Arla stepped down from the robot's arms and walked into the room. She ignored the woman and turned to her father with her arms open. She embraced him and, after a moment, he relaxed, all anger gone.

"Sorry, father, I wanted one last look before the choosing."

Jabe patted her back and they separated. "You know I worry when you go alone, there are many hazards on the path up the mountain and you've only just returned before curfew."

She smiled at him. His anger had been a cloak for his fear, as always. "I didn't mean for you to worry. I knew R.DJ would come after me."

"I suppose you'll be wanting something to eat, though it's past dining hour," said the sour-faced woman.

Arla turned to her. "Yes please..." she said. Then after a moment, she added the word she knew her father wanted to hear. "...mother." The woman was nothing of the sort, but she'd been assigned to the family when Jabe's wife had died as he was of good stock and still fertile. Her half-brother lay asleep in the room he shared with Arla. The room that had been hers.

It was hard to say whether there was any affection between the two of them. Companionship, perhaps, but her stepmother, whose name was Becca, didn't possess a personality it was easy to like. If, indeed, she could be said to possess a personality at all. Becca had come into the family believing she would be able to take charge, based, no doubt, on Jabe's placid nature and reputation for being a good, honest, man. But she'd found, soon enough, that, while Jabe was all those things, he was also as solid as wrought iron and just as easy to bend. Though he spoke rarely, everyone knew that what he said he meant, whether in the privacy of his own home or in the world at large.

Jabe sat next to Arla at the large wooden table in the kitchen of the timber farmhouse. In the orange glow of the oil lamps hung above the mantelpiece and in front of the window, he regarded his daughter as she tucked greedily into the stew that had been deposited carelessly under her nose by Becca.

"What did you see? Was it good viewing tonight?" he asked, eagerly.

Becca slammed a goblet onto the table beside him and began filling it from a bottle. "You ain't got no right askin' her that, Jabe Farmer. She shouldn't 'ave been up there and that's a fact. That there is a holy place and the likes of her ain't to see it, not else she gets chosen tomorrow. Though fat chance of that."

"Still your tongue," Jabe said in a voice of calm command. "Do you forget that it was me who showed her where it was? That it was alonger me that she saw the other side for the first time?"

"Now just you stop right there, husband. You shouldn't 'ave done it then and she shouldn't be doing it now. That mountain has filled you with strange notions and it's done you no good at all."

"You don't have to listen to us talk, wife. Make yourself comfortable in the front room and we'll be out presently." Jabe smiled at Arla as Becca huffed out, chuntering to herself as she went.

"It was awesome, pa," Arla said as soon as her stepmother had disappeared. "I saw more fires than ever, it looked as though the whole of the far side was alight!"

Jabe smiled. "I wish I could have come with you. I'll slip away some time and take another look, just to convince myself it's still there."

Arla leaned in and laid her hand on her father's arm. "So, what do you think causes the lights? You've never said. When you showed me the first time, you told me you didn't know and so wouldn't guess. But I know you won't have stopped thinking about it."

"True enough. I said less than I believed at the time because it'd be called blasphemy by some. The dogma says that up there is where purgatory lies and the little lights you see are souls burning in torment."

This sort of talk made Arla uncomfortable. Her father was an unconventional man who kept his own council, but if Becca got wind of his wild theories then as sure as rocks are rocks, she'd inform on her husband. Jabe would be excommunicated or imprisoned. They might even inflict one of the old punishments on him. Arla shuddered - but she had to know.

"But you don't believe the dogma, do you dad?" she whispered.

Jabe shook his head. "No. Seems to me that what we see when we look up beyond the sky in those few minutes after dusk, is pretty much exactly what anyone looking back at us would see. Now, it might be some weird reflection off the atmosphere, but I don't think so. It looks too real to me and the lights don't appear in the right places. Sometimes there are fires lit over there but not on our side. No, it seems to me that the circling sea doesn't lead to purgatory, and neither does it mark the edge of the world. It's just what separates us from whoever is dancing round those lights."

"Yes, that's what I think too, though it seems impossible."

"Impossible? No, but it goes against everything we're taught from childhood," Jabe said, speaking in low, but urgent, tones. "Everyone knows the world was made by God when she ploughed a furrow out of the primordial rocks and planted her garden there. We call it the valley and all people live within its bounds. God poured waters at each side of the valley and they soar up, forming a magical wall that keeps out the demons of the night. We know that wall of water exists because we can see it from the valley. We know that if we took a boat from the valley's lip, we could sail that ocean, but that if we did, we would pass into purgatory where the sinful souls wait.

But what if that's all a lie? Not the geography: we can see that our world is shaped like a tube with our own eyes. No, I mean, what if all the explanations are lies? What if, on the other side of this tube, there's another valley just like ours where they're fed the same dogma and banned from looking at us, let alone finding us?"

Arla withdrew her hands and leaned back. "Why are you telling me this dad? Why now?"

"Because the ceremony is tomorrow and you might be chosen."

"Me! Chosen to be a priest? You're crazy!"

Smiling, Jabe took her hand. "No, love. It's true that when I was a lad we knew who was for the priesthood before the ceremony even took place. It was the devout ones, the ones who would learn their scripture and repeat it. The ones who lived the life of an acolyte before they even became one."

"Yes, that's what I heard. And at the last ceremony, five years ago, didn't they take Navendu, Petra and Nix? They were the most pious little shits I ever met."

"Watch your language," snapped Jabe, "you're not an adult yet. But yes, they took those three. And they also took Andriea and Jak, the two brightest kids I've ever met. Excepting you, of course." He gave a rueful smile.

Arla stood up and stepped away from the table. She began absentmindedly fiddling with the ornaments there, selecting the Ring of God for particular attention. "You're right, pa. And don't think I hadn't noticed who they chose last time, I just imagined it was something random or maybe that Andriea and Jak were more devout than I thought. But I can't be a priest! That would mean leaving you and everyone I know."

From the table, Jabe looked at her standing with her back to him. He felt a lump in his throat - was it pride or sadness? Or both? "No, you wouldn't come back to live here, but you might visit if you want, there's nothing in the Coda that says you can't."

"But no-one ever does," said Arla, turning round and meeting her father's gaze. "Something happens to them that means they lose all their memories of their childhood and home, or maybe they're changed so they no longer care."

"That's true, my darling Arla, but they weren't you. If you're chosen tomorrow, I have faith that you'll do the right thing by your family and that I'll see you again."

Arla didn't speak, but she moved back to the table and fell into her father's arms. She'd never heard him speak of faith before, at least not as a good thing. He was a man who trusted in things he could see, touch and understand. Faith was for the desperate, he'd said.

They held each other until she fell asleep. The next day, the priests came and she was chosen.

The Training

DATE: FIRST CONTACT minus 2 years

Arla stood beside Brother Elias as he performed the rite of joining. As a novice, she wasn't permitted to take an active part in the ceremony, still less to use the holy instruments, but she was, nevertheless, treated with reverence by the common folk gathered around them.

She didn't like Elias, though she'd been told it was a sin to judge others. He was a rigid, arrogant cleric of around 50 years, rumoured to have reduced every novice he'd ever been assigned to tears. His tactics hadn't worked on her, they'd done no more than induce a deep loathing that she did her best to hide. She wasn't sure she was entirely successful.

The whole settlement was here. Cluster 551 was an agri-chemical facility which meant, in essence, that it made fertiliser out of crap. It also stunk and so Arla used all the meditative skills she'd learned over the past three years to block out the overwhelming stench of cattle and human dung. The people gathered around the ceremony stone didn't seem to notice, though. Three families had babies ready for the joining and Elias had spent the past ten minutes lecturing them in the required way. They had renounced the devil and all her minions and vowed to protect their children from the forces of evil.

Arla gazed up at the sky as she considered what evil actually was. After three years at priest school, she'd come to the conclusion that evil meant anything new or different, anything outside the dogma. Of course there was murder, jealousy and theft, everyone knew about them, but it seemed to her that the priesthood cared more about deviation from the word and laws of the Goddess than anything she would recognise as being truly evil.

She sighed as she tried to see through the blue sky to the people she knew to be beyond. She hadn't forgotten that last night on top of the mountain, or her father's words. But neither had she been to see him. At first, they'd been banned from visiting their family. Something to do with adjusting to the fact that, as priests, everyone was their family and no-one was. After the end of her second year, the ban had been lifted but still she hadn't gone to visit home. For some reason, she felt as though to do so would be to invite scrutiny of him, and her, and the last thing she wanted was for the brotherhood to take an interest in her unconventional father.

Elias was now using the Naming Wand. She had to concede that he was a consummate showman. He'd made the relatively simple process of entering the child's identity details into the wand seem to be some sort of mystic ceremony. Which was, of course, the entire point. She'd noticed this about her training. Much of it was reinforcing the students' knowledge of the dogma, of course, but, more than anything else, she'd been taught how to carry out each of the major ceremonies and how to use the holy instruments properly. She'd been a little disappointed when she'd first been handed a Naming Wand as she'd imagined it would *feel* holy in some way. But it was just a rod of metal with a row of buttons on the back and she'd then spent several months learning how to use it properly.

"And so I welcome thee, Narsi Petrovic Technician, to God's community in this her sacred valley."

Arla watched as Elias brought the wand down and pressed it to the space between the baby's shoulder blades as it was held, naked, in the arms of its mother. The wand erupted into a dazzling sequence of colours and holy music played, almost entirely covering up the child's squeals as Elias pressed the hidden button that ended the ceremony. As a novice, Arla wasn't yet permitted to know what exactly the button did, beyond, that is, the standard dogma that it made the child a spiritual link in the chain that bound the people of the whole world together. But whatever the true purpose of the wand, it hurt the child, even if only for a few moments. It left a pinprick mark on the child's back which they bore for the rest of their lives, as she bore hers.

The other two children were brought forward, formally named, and had the wand applied to them with the same combination of colour, music and screaming. Parents beamed and cringed in equal measure, the gathered community clapped their approval. And Arla watched it all with a sort of detached interest that she found worrying. She'd been an acolyte for two years and yet she felt no more a priest than she had when she was chosen. Oh, she had learned the rituals she'd been taught and could recite the key canticles, she'd listened to the lessons of the tutor priest and even witnessed the lesser miracles. She had seen, with her own eyes, how a farmer who was so sick she could barely walk was cured by a single application of a holy instrument as well as countless other demonstrations of the power she would obtain when she graduated. And yet she felt nothing.

She woke from her reverie when Elias tugged on the sleeve of her cassock. Of course, the ceremony was over and the people were waiting for the priests to leave. She mumbled an apology and followed Elias out of the chapel, out onto a sunlit lawn and into the village hall. His pace was so slow that Arla had to hold herself back from overtaking him, but the reason soon became clear as, along the far wall of the little hall, the local leaders awaited them. Arla suppressed a chuckle as the little fat man, who turned out to be the plant governor, and the thin old woman, attempted to appear composed as they fought to find their breath. She imagined, in her mind's eye, the old girl and the fat man running out of the chapel's side door and into the hall's back door while the priests were dawdling. Traditions really were stupid sometimes.

An hour later, Arla found herself cornered by the man she'd originally found so amusing but now couldn't escape. His name was Feng Li and he clearly took great pride in the efficient running of the plant. He'd been obviously upset to be talking to the novice rather than the priest, but he'd warmed up under her polite and interested questioning. Well, pretending to be interested was, of course, essential when training to be a priest.

Her rescue came along with an overwhelming stench as Feng's gaze focused on a point about her left shoulder. "What are you doing here R.SH?"

Arla spun round to find herself looking up at a robot of humanoid form except for the addition of a second set of arms that sprung from its torso.

"I am sorry, master Feng, but there has been an accident. Technician Shi Tu has fallen into a supply vat."

"By the mother!" Feng cried, "Where is she now?"

"I retrieved her, master Feng, but she is not breathing. I fear she has ingested the supply fluid."

Elias had been attracted to the commotion as a fly to manure. Feng turned to him. "You must help!" he said.

After a moment, Elias said: "Novice Arla will help. She has been trained in the proper ceremonies."

Panic flooded Arla's stomach. What did he mean? Why wasn't he going to treat the woman, he who usually wanted as much attention as possible. She allowed herself to be guided out of the hall's back door and out onto the concrete pavement behind. This was an industrial sector so, away from the chapel with its grass lawn, it was an unattractive huddle of metal and concrete buildings around a large plant. She found herself looking down at a figure prone and unmoving. It was completely soaked with liquid excrement - so that was the supply fluid the robot mentioned and this was why Elias was so keen to take a back seat.

"Please help!" said one of the men gathered around the body. She seemed to be the only one here with a sense of smell, but she swallowed it, and the vomit that was rising into her gullet, and knelt down beside the body.

"Get me a bucket of water!" she shouted. Within moments it appeared hanging from the arm of the robot. "Tip it over her."

"I cannot, mistress. That would cause harm to mistress Shi."

Arla jumped to her feet. "Give it to me," she said, snatching the bucket from the robot. She emptied its contents over the woman and stepped back as a pool of diluted slurry spread across the pavement. She'd hoped this might shock the woman, but it had no effect other than to clean off some of the sludge. The men and women gathered around her began babbling - some shouting, some crying.

What should she do? Calm. In amongst all this noise, she had to find peace. Now, search. The woman's lungs were clearly blocked. What was the correct ritual? It couldn't involve a holy instrument because Elias only had the Naming Wand with him and it would be blasphemous to use that for the wrong purpose. No. Think. Think.

Arla knelt down beside the woman's body and, holding back the wave of nausea, rolled her onto her front, then, straddling her back she pushed hard down on the woman's rib cage. Once, twice, three times. A river of brown sludge erupted from Shi's throat and Arla flipped her onto her back again.She ripped a piece of fabric from her cassock and used it to wipe Shi's face before drawing in a deep breath and blowing into her mouth. She watched as Shi's lungs inflated, then pulled away as her chest compressed again. She did it again. The third time, panic, as well as bile, was flooding her body. Her head was swimming, but she drew in a final breath and blew into Shi's mouth. Her chest rose and she gave a tremendous heave and coughed up another batch of sludge.

Rolling the woman onto her side, Arla thumped her back as Shi coughed and sucked in one breath, then another. Her arms flailed as she coughed, flecks of blood showing among the sewage. She turned onto her back and opened her eyes. She was crying, but she was alive.

"You have saved her!" cried one man as the gathered crowd erupted in cheers, all of the composure they usually showed around a priest gone in that instant.

Arla stood up and was lost in a sea of arms tugging at her, faces crying and laughing, eyes full of tears. She had performed her first miracle.

"You are truly a breather of life," Governor Feng said once he'd forced his way through the crowd. He watched as Shi Tu was carried away by her colleagues and, having shaken Arla's hand and given a brief bow, he followed them.

Arla turned to Elias who had watched the whole affair from a distance. The smile died on her lips when she saw his face. "You are a disgrace to the priesthood. Look at you," he snarled, "your cassock torn and covered in filth. Where is your dignity?"

"But I saved her! It was the only way," she protested feebly.

"Better to have let her die than to disgrace the priesthood. I will make a full report on this, believe me. This will be your last day as a novice if I have any say in the matter. Now, come with me!"

Arla followed the priest dejectedly towards the transport, hardly noticing the cheers as it took off and headed into the sky. She had done what she thought was right, what she thought Elias was expecting her to do. Or did he expect her to fail? Had she been a sacrifice to preserve his reputation? If she'd failed, after all, it would have been her fault not his. The more she thought about it, the more she knew she was right. The slimy bastard had set her up. Fail and she would lose status and possibly not qualify, succeed and he would say she'd betrayed the priesthood.

She was confined to the cargo hold as the transport made its way to the priest level, the stench being too great for either Elias or the pilot to bear. They were met by two robots who gently but firmly took her away and showered her before incinerating her cassock. She accepted all this without protest because she knew Elias was correct. This would be her last day as a novice priest.

And she was right.

The Engineer

SHE FELT UNUSUALLY groggy when she awoke, as if she'd been drinking alcohol – something she hadn't done since she was admitted into the Seminary. Then she noticed that her hands were tied and when she looked up in panic she saw a ceiling she didn't recognise. She tried to cry out, but her mouth was gagged. What had happened? She'd gone to sleep in her usual bed and her only concern had been Elias's reaction to the miracle she had performed the previous day.

What had seemed a crisis the night before was swept away in the adrenaline of waking up in a strange sterile bed, in a strange sterile environment. A gentle hum was all she could hear and the air smelled of warm dust.

The door opened and a robot came in, but it was a robot such as she had never seen before. Even the household robots such as R.DJ, whilst humanoid in general shape, had proportions that were more suited to their role as servants and workers on the farms and industrial units that scattered the valley. This robot, on the other hand, was more like a walking mannequin, the kind of fake human made of what looked like plastic and metal. Its eyes weren't hidden behind the sort of protective band that ran horizontally around the top of the head of robots like R.DJ, this robot's eyes were perfectly proportioned and exactly the same size as those of an adult man, although obviously artificial.

The robot entered the room, and strode over to the bed. Its lifeless eyes looked down at her with the same faint flickering she'd seen in those of R.DJ when he was carrying out a stressful task. His metal hand touched her arm and he paused as if he were a doctor taking a pulse, then he raised his arm, turned around and wordlessly strode from the room.

Arla watched as he went. The room she was in seemed to be made of metal and contained no furniture save the panel attached to the wall above her head. She couldn't see what the panel contained, but she got the impression of colours and pulsing lights, as if someone was painting it and then rubbing out their markings in time with her heartbeat.

She let her head drop into the soft pillow and forced air in through her nose, trying her best to breathe deeply and relax as she'd been taught during her priest training. Where was she? Her only theory was that she was being punished for whatever she'd done the day before, though she honestly couldn't understand how saving that woman's life could possibly be a cause for sanction. Her only option was to relax and wait for her punishment.

She didn't have to wait for long as, only a few minutes after the robot had left, the door opened again, this time admitting a woman. She was small, middle-aged and sported a greying blonde bob of hair shorter than would be considered decent amongst Arla's farming community. The woman strode confidently in, followed by the robot she'd seen earlier who remained beside the door as if he were her protector. She didn't look like any priest that Arla had ever seen, she looked more like the scribes that worked in the chemical factories tallying the batches, or the tax collectors that brought their clipboards and pens at harvest time.

"I'm sorry about this," she said. "Every time we do this I tell them that gagging is not necessary, after all who you going to call out to? My name is Dr Indira McCall and I'm going to take the gag out now – please do not shout."

The cloth was swept from her face but it was a few breathless moments before Arla could speak. "Where am I?"

"Well, now, that question will need to wait a little to be answered in full," McCall said, with apparently genuine sympathy, "too much information too quickly can be dangerous. Suffice it to say that you are safe, completely safe. I know it's hard, but I ask you to trust me - I have your best interests at heart."

"Am I in trouble? Because of disobeying Father Elias?"

McCall shook her head. "No, indeed not! You have passed the test and have graduated."

"As a priest? Is this the inner sanctum where the miracles are revealed?" Arla managed, her head swimming.

"No, I think it's fair to say that you're not cut out to be a priest," McCall responded with a warm smile. "You, my dear, are to be an engineer."

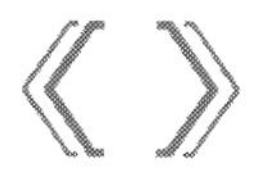

FOR TWO DAYS ARLA REMAINED in that room. Her restraints had been removed and she'd been asked not to venture outside. She felt as though this was a test, just like the one she'd passed by chance by saving that sewage worker. But what was the correct response? Should she try to escape? Were they waiting to see if she had the initiative to get away? Or were they testing whether she could be trusted to follow orders? Paralysed by the choice, she decided to stay put because she had no clue where she was - she needed more information before making a break for it.

Robots, much like the first, came and went, bringing food and some books she'd asked for. The only human being she saw was Dr McCall, though she got the impression of movement from the corridor outside whenever the doctor entered the room.

Arla found herself settling into her new environment. She no longer noticed the dusty smell or the sterile lighting. She examined the room minutely. The walls were white though, here and there, they'd suffered damage - scuffs and dents mainly. The floor was a shiny black plastic that her feet left no trace on. Half way up the walls and spaced evenly around the room were small square panels that extruded slightly from the surface. Each had an identical complement of circular and rectangular recesses that looked like those that accepted the holy instruments. There were eight of these panels and Arla guessed that the room could hold up to that many beds although, right now, hers was the only one here. The bed itself was made of plastic. It was clean and comfortable but, when she examined it closely, it bore the marks of age.

McCall had brought her clothes to wear. An outer suit of shirt and trousers in a blue so pure and deep she wondered how they had been made. The clothes felt smoother and yet more rigid than those she was used to at home and as an acolyte.

There was also a glass ball embedded in the ceiling. She'd never seen anything like it, but she felt as though it were an artificial eye, watching her. Each morning, when it was time to dress, she pushed the bed away from the wall and put on her underwear behind its cover.

She tensed as she heard the familiar sound of footsteps approaching the door, and the gentle puff of its locking mechanism. Dr McCall stepped in. Under her arm she carried a bundle of folded clothes which she placed on the bed with some ceremony. "This is your uniform and these..." she said, dropping a pair of black boots on top, "are your shoes. Are you ready to see what's outside this door?"

McCall reflected back Arla's beaming smile. "Those clothes you have on now are for use during leisure hours, you can leave them here and I'll have them taken to your quarters. Your uniform should fit well enough, but it can be adjusted if necessary." She turned and left the room, closing the door behind her. This time, the locking mechanism was not activated.

Arla unfolded the uniform. It was of a deep blue that flirted with black, the only accent being a strip of reflective cloth that ran up the outside of each leg and arm. The cloth felt much more dense than the light cotton trousers and tops she was used to, closer to priestly vestments but of obviously higher quality. There was a one-piece top that she pulled over her head, breathing in a sharp, nasal, aroma that she thought must be the dye, and smoothed it down her torso. The top seemed to expand and contract as she breathed without feeling at all restrictive, and the trousers, which were made of the same material, also hugged her legs in a warm, pleasant, way.

She looked at herself in the mirror. Even though she was twenty years old, her pencil-like body shape and the short hair she'd worn as a priest left her looking more like a pubescent boy. But these were, without doubt, the finest clothes she'd ever worn and, on her left shoulder, shone a golden emblem, somehow woven into the fabric. She moved closer to the mirror to get a better look. It was a rising sun.

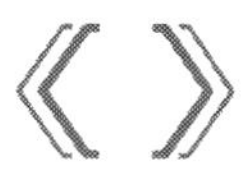

ARLA OPENED THE DOOR a crack, then, when nothing catastrophic happened, a little more. Her door opened onto a whitewashed corridor. Dr McCall stood against the wall watching her as Arla looked left and right. The corridor stretched for some way to the left and right, with doors at regular intervals on both sides and at each end. She swung around at the familiar puff and a face peered back at her from what was, presumably, another room like hers. The face was of a girl of around her age, but the first thing Arla noticed was her skin, which was of a rich chestnut, and her thick, tightly curled, hair.

"This is Kiama," Dr McCall said, gesturing at the other girl. "She arrived just before you. We don't usually have two to orient at the same time, but it is probably no bad thing. Come Kiama Mchungaji, do not be afraid."

The girl edged out of her room and Arla could see that she was dressed in exactly the same way, down to the sunrise on her shoulder. Arla smiled in a way she hoped was reassuring.

"Where are you from?" Kiama said.

At first, Arla struggled to understand what she said. Kiama spoke with an accent that was very different to hers and, indeed, Dr McCall's. It was thick and sonorous with more expression of the vowels than Arla had ever heard. She'd met people from all over the valley, but they all spoke in much the same way. Then a thought hit her. "Are you from beyond the sky?"

Kiama paused. Was it because she didn't understand Arla's words or was it the meaning? After all, Arla herself wasn't entirely sure of what she was saying.

"You will find out the answer to that question and many others very soon, Apprentice," McCall said to Arla. "Very soon indeed. Now, I think it's time I showed you where you truly are."

She strode to the door at the end of the corridor, turned the handle and swung it open.

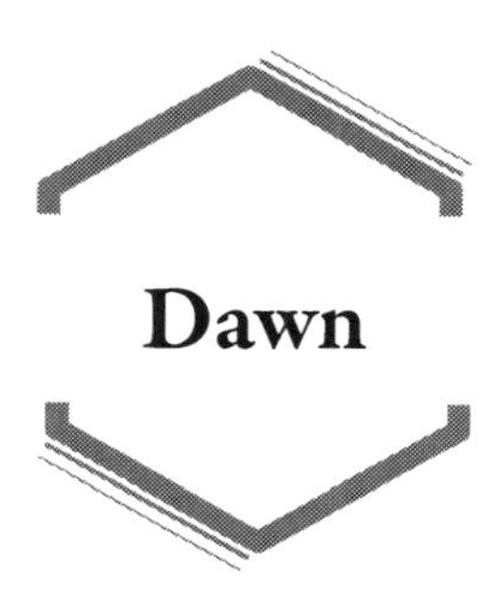

Dawn

THE CORRIDOR FILLED with the chatter of a watching crowd that fell into silence as the door slid open and Dr McCall stepped through.

Arla could see, beyond her, a gaggle of people straining to see down the corridor. Most were dressed in uniforms like hers, although the dark blue had faded to varying degrees. Arla crept forward to the threshold of the door, her eyes drawn to these people. There were perhaps three dozen men and women, all adults, though most of them young with only a few grey-hairs like the doctor.

"Come," McCall said, waving to Arla. "Come and meet your crewmates."

Arla stepped nervously through and, as she did so, the crowd began to applaud and she could make out cries of welcome and encouragement. They were gathered in a large room. No, it was a corridor, much bigger than the one she'd emerged from and running at right angles to it. Aside from the people, it was the walls she noticed first - an almost continuous row of portraits of people in uniforms, and each had a brass dedication.

She turned to Kiama and held out her hand. The girl took it and stepped through, flinching from the applause that grew even louder when she appeared.

The doctor raised her hands in what was obviously a well understood signal and the people fell silent and melted away, their clanky footsteps fading away until the corridor was empty except for the three of them.

"When you stepped through that door, you became crew."

"But what are *crew*?" Arla asked.

McCall smiled. "You have heard of the Engineers? The ones who visit the valley during curfew?"

Both girls nodded.

"The crew are the Engineers. You will become them too."

Arla shook her head passionately. "No, the Engineers are holy. We learned that in the valley and I was taught it during my training to be a priest."

"Me also," Kiama said. "And I have seen them - they can fly without wings and without ships, no person can do that."

Smiling, McCall said: "I understand this is hard for you. Much of what you see in the coming days will challenge what you have been taught. You will understand why you were told those things about the crew, but for now, come with me and I will begin your training."

The doctor set off along the deserted corridor, the only sound the metallic thud of her boots on the floor, the two girls scampering along beside her, desperate not to be left alone in this alien place. The corridor ended in a wall and in that wall was a panel that, when McCall pressed her hand to it, slid open.

Inside was a small room with no obvious exit other than the one they'd just stepped through. There was some sort of lit decoration on one of the otherwise bare walls except for what looked like handles placed on the walls and ceiling, there were even recessed grips in the floor.

"Bio tunnel observation," McCall said.

"Acknowledged, Bio tunnel observation deck. ETA one hundred and thirty-five seconds." The voice seemed to come from everywhere and, though the words themselves were clear enough, they were delivered in a flat, emotionless, voice. Like that of a robot.

Arla was about to open her mouth when the room began to move. It was a subtle shift to her balance and there were no visual signs - except that the lit decoration she'd noticed began to spread across the wall, as if it were following the room's progress.

"This is called a pod. It's a small room, like a sort of enclosed cart, that runs on rails so that we can get to places that are not otherwise easy to reach."

There was nothing to say to this because Arla didn't really understand a word of it. She still had no idea where she was.

After a few moments, she began to feel a little unsteady, as if the blood were draining from her feet, and she put her hand out to touch the wall.

"Yes, you will feel a little odd," the doctor said when she noticed this, "I won't explain it yet, but you'll feel lighter and lighter until, soon, you will have no weight at all. You'll find the handles useful soon."

Sure enough, Arla felt as though her body were becoming lighter. It was as if the transporter were filling with water - the only time she'd experienced anything like it was when she'd been swimming in Oxbow Lake. She looked across at Kiama who stood, with eyes wide, as she lifted each foot, as if testing whether they really were lighter. She gave a shriek and Arla went to comfort her, but her cry hadn't been born of fear, the girl was delighted.

Then, quite suddenly, Arla felt her feet lift and she was floating. She reached for a handle, her palm slamming into the cold metal wall and sending her reeling away to collide with the opposite side of the room a few moments later. A strong hand grasped her arm and she turned her head to see McCall, one hand on a rail and the other on her. Kiama, meanwhile, was doing somersaults.

"I feel sick" Arla said.

McCall pulled Arla towards her. "Grab that handle," she said before dipping her hand into her pocket and bringing out a small plastic box that she flipped open. She opened a flap and a tiny circular pill floated out. "Here, swallow this. I came prepared."

Arla grabbed the pill and swallowed just as the pod came to a gentle halt.

"Give it a moment and it'll be better," McCall said with a smile. "And don't worry, weightlessness affects most people that way the first time."

"Not her, though," Arla managed, waving a hand in Kiama's general direction.

"Yes, she's a natural."

Kiama came to a halt, floating gently in front of the doctor and Arla. "It's wonderful," she said, "like swimming only better!"

"Well, now it's time for me to show you what we've come to see, but before we do, tell me Kiama where it is you come from."

The young woman's dark face hardened. "I don't know what you mean. There is only the valley."

"And you, Arla, where do you come from?"

"Everyone comes from the valley."

McCall nodded as she floated. "And have you ever seen anyone with skin like Kiama's?"

"No, I haven't."

The doctor turned to the other girl. "And Kiama, have you seen anyone with skin the colour of ours?"

Kiama shook her head. "No, I thought you were sick when I first saw you. And then I saw there were others and I didn't understand."

"Well now you will," McCall said. "Open the pod door."

"Acknowledged," the robot voice said and, with a hiss, the door they'd entered through opened onto darkness.

The doctor put her hand on Arla's shoulder. "Careful now, go hand over hand."

Arla floated inexpertly through the open portal and into another enclosed space, wider than the pod but still smaller than the room she'd been in. The chamber was only illuminated by the light from the pod so it faded into total darkness to the left and right. Arla grabbed the handrail on the wall opposite the door, coming to rest alongside Kiama.

"It will be dark for a moment when I close the pod door, do not be afraid," McCall said from behind them. And yet, despite the warning, it was all Arla could do to stop herself from crying out as she heard the hiss and the chamber went black.

"Open observation hatch one 10%."

"Acknowledged."

A horizontal strip of light appeared at eye level and Arla could immediately see that the wall in front of them was covered in a shutter that was now opening from the centre. The brightness filled the chamber and Arla screwed her eyes up until, carefully, she opened them a crack and looked through the gap in the wall.

Her first impression was of green to left and right, blue above and below. It was all curved, as if she were looking down the inside of a huge tunnel. Immediately in front of her, dead centre of the tunnel, was a black circle surrounded by a bright white halo.

"What do you see?" McCall said. "Look at the green. Look closely."

Arla focused her gaze on the green strip to her left. She could see that it wasn't of one uniform colour - there were dark browns and greys running in a line up the middle of the strip and dotted here and there small patches of blue. Then she recognised it.

"It looks like the valley, but from impossibly high up. I've seen these colours from above, but never this distant."

"Yes, that is exactly what you are seeing," McCall said, obviously pleased. "To the left is the place you call the valley, Arla, and to the right is your valley, Kiama."

Kiama, who'd remained completely still and silent as her eyes drank in the scene, shook her head. "How can this be? There is only one valley. It was created by the Goddess."

"No, this is what you must understand. There are two - Arla's we call the North Valley and yours is called the South. And they weren't built by any Goddess. They were built by people, by your ancestors and mine, many hundreds of years ago. They built this world so that we could find another, one big enough to fill. No child quotas, no population control at all. Our mission is to build a new Earth," McCall said, her words tumbling out, "but we cannot succeed. Others have got there before us."

Arla turned away from the view to face McCall. "I don't understand most of what you just said. What is this *Earth*? How can people build a world?"

"What? Oh, you'd be surprised at what people can achieve. For now, I ask you to believe me or, at least, be open-minded. You can see the two valleys and between them the seas. They are set within a tunnel carved out of the inside of a huge ball of rock."

"But what stops all the people falling?" Kiama asked.

"The rock is spinning at just the right speed to keep them firmly on the ground without excessive weight. We are weightless because we are precisely at the axis of rotation. The black disk covers the end of a tube that runs the length of the tunnel - when you lived in the valleys, you called it the sun and the disc protects us from blindness and incineration as we stand here."

"And Earth? What is that?" Arla said.

Doctor McCall smiled. "It is our home, where our ancestors came from. But it was dying and this little world is like a seed, flying across the universe to settle a new planet. Except, somehow, we find others here before us and they don't seem friendly. The people of the valleys don't know any of this, but soon their innocence will be broken, as yours has, and they may be asked to help us fight for our survival."

EVA

OUTLINE: MISSION DAWN
OBJECTIVE: Preserve the species by seeding a new world on the nearest habitable planet in the absence of any breakthrough in faster-than-light travel.
METHOD: Carve out a habitation tunnel within a nickel-rich asteroid. Seal it and build a working eco-system to include approximately 2,000 human settlers plus 50 crew. Use ion drive to accelerate to 0.05 the speed of light.
MISSION LENGTH: Approximately 1450 years

DATE: FIRST CONTACT

Arla gave the sensor array a final wipe and waved to those she knew to be watching through the newly cleaned camera lens. She now had a few moments to simply enjoy being where she was, just as when she'd laid on her back and looked at the sky all those years ago. She now knew, of course, that she really had seen people on the other side of the sky - they were the inhabitants of Valley South - though she'd only been able to do so because the lighting technology was showing signs of age. She also knew that she was on a rotating ball of rock heading towards the star that was supposed to be their home, but that now, it seemed, held danger. And she knew that suns are spheres not tubes. But knowing all this did nothing to still the sense of *wrongness* about it all.

She turned her back on the bunker, all dark pitted metal and transparent aluminium, and gazed upon the surface of the asteroid. The whole ship was officially called *Dawn*, but undertaking an EVA was *going rockside* and so here she was, rocking it.

The tiny sun of the system they were heading for leapt over the horizon and she staggered in the sudden light as her suit fans whined into action. She pulled down her visor and looked again as the star slowly arced its way from right to left, the whole landscape seeming to shift as pitch black shadows moved beneath pure white boulders.

Her earpiece buzzed into life. "Arla, the boss says it's time to come in."

"Ki, you're breaking up," Arla responded, theatrically thumping the side of her helmet.

She could hear giggling. "Careful, that helmet's so old it might just crack. And anyway, I know what you're up to and you'd better be quick. You'll be on basic rations for a week as it is, so you might as well go for it."

Arla waved and headed carefully for the railcar. Dawn's spin was so fast and gravity so weak that it'd be all too easy to step down too hard and go careering off, with no hope of any help. So the surface had been fitted with steel rails and cars to travel them. Arla was tethered and she tiptoed carefully back towards the safety of the transport. She chuckled as she remembered her first EVA, over a year ago now, when she'd shot off the surface and had been brought back by her supervisor - he in the railcar and her bobbing along on her tether like a metallic balloon. She doubted she'd been the first to suffer this humiliation, but that didn't stop the ribbing she got when she returned. She'd been "Floats" ever since.

She sat in the car and punched down on the simple matrix of buttons on its console. She wasn't going back inside just yet, there was something she wanted to see. The car jerked into motion, taking her further from the safety of the dome. As it moved onto tracks that hadn't been used in years, it began to vibrate. Adrenaline surged into Arla's stomach and she almost leapt off but, once the button was pressed, the car would continue on its journey and she didn't fancy being stranded out here and having to creep back. She'd also have to explain why the car had been left at the end of the track and how she planned to retrieve it. No, she was in enough trouble as it was, she would see it through.

It took a minute or so. A minute spent listening to her own breathing and the hum of the railcar transmitted through the suit. A brief moment, entirely alone, contemplating the universe as she cast her eyes upwards into its stark blackness.

The end of the track was set in what looked like a refuse heap, presumably of some mining or construction operation. As soon as the car stopped, she climbed off, careful in her excitement and haste to step slowly, moving her feet in the odd sort of forward-only gait she'd been taught in training.

She'd been told it was over the little dust hill. She climbed, a little piece of her wondering whether this was nothing more than an elaborate joke dressed up as a myth. If so, the balloon humiliation would be nothing compared to the ribbing she'd get for falling for it.

She reached the top and scanned the foot of the heap, her heart pounding. It wasn't there. Yes it was! The sun that by now was beginning its descent from noon glinted off something shiny and rectangular. She almost leapt for joy, and stopped herself just in time. This would make the perfect launching point if she never wanted to see her friends again. Instead, she scrambled carefully down the slope and, when she reached the bottom, knelt beside the object.

It was cuboid and stood slightly askew on spindly legs that were buried in the soil. On the top, a dish array pointed into the cosmos like an eye popping out between the solar panels that covered its body. She touched it with a gloved hand and found what she'd been looking for. On the front, barely readable in the reflected light of her suit, was the inscription: "CERES XV: SURVEY MISSION 2315". This was a relic of the distant past, when her ancient ancestors had first been looking for a suitable vessel to house this splinter of humanity. It was the Ceres XV mission that had identified this as the place and it had been left undisturbed through the entire construction phase, even when all the terraformers with their massive machines had gone. It had been sitting there waiting for the boldest.

There was one more thing to do. Arla stood and examined the inside of the communications dish. There it was, the markings scratched into the metal by the first to rediscover it centuries ago. She read the characters twice and ran them over in her mind until she was sure she'd remember them. Then she scrambled carefully up the slope again before, with a quick look over her shoulder as she reached the top, she headed for the car.

"Engineer Grade 2 Arla Mirova, you are hereby found guilty of an unauthorised deviation from mission plan and are sentenced to minimum rations for seven days."

Arla sighed. "Yes sir," she said and got back into the car.

SHE SAT WITH AN EQUAL mix of pride and anger as the car trundled its way back over the landscape of whites and blacks towards the bunker. She had achieved what few had dared to achieve, she'd read the words on the communications dish. And her reward (apart from the admiration of her peers) was a week eating biscuits and drinking water. But she had no regrets. As soon as she'd been told of the ancient probe and the secret writing it bore she resolved to find it and hang the consequences.

On the other hand, it seemed unfair that initiative and boldness were punished by the powers that be. But then what did she expect from officers who hid behind vid-links in their hermetically sealed quarters? The engineers were selected from the people of the valleys, but command positions were passed down from father to son, mother to daughter. A pathological fear of infection had also been bred into the officer class and so she'd never personally met any of them and neither had any of her crew-mates. Orders were passed electronically and supervised by senior NCO's - like Kiama, who'd excelled at everything since she'd started training. Arla, on the other hand, had proven to be a competent engineer but, as she'd yet again demonstrated, also a loose canon.

The chief puzzle, for Arla and her fellow recruits, was how such a small cadre of officers retained any sort of genetic diversity. And they *were* diverse. The engineers were evenly split between the light brown skinned Valley Northers and the dark brown skinned Valley Southers, though, admittedly, with variations in skin tone. It was rare indeed for a Northerner to be mistaken for a Southerner and this had been explained by the nature of the initial populations of the valleys - one was derived from the northern hemisphere of Earth and the other from the southern. The officers, on the other hand, were startlingly diverse. Her current nemesis, Lieutenant Commander Patel, had a round face of a deep browny-yellow whereas Lieutenant Murphy's skin seemed to contain no colour at all. Various theories had been floated, the most plausible of which was that they had some sort of egg or embryo store that they used to replace officers, but this would require the sort of precision timing of human fertility that was impossible to imagine. And she'd never seen a pregnant officer.

She cogitated on this as the car continued its slow journey back. And so it was that she didn't notice the space ship coming silently in to land until she was overwhelmed by the dust-storm from its thrusters.

The Mock Empress

HER IMPERIAL MAJESTY, Victorea, Ruler of the Vanis Federation and Guardian of the Faith scowled as the tiresome man bobbed and sweated before her.

"Spit it out, Lavar!" she shrieked, her notoriously low patience threshold long ago exceeded. "Or shall I show mercy and spare you the effort, since I know what you're going to say."

The man fawned and his tonsured head sparkled in the light of the chandeliers as he bowed.

Victorea gave a grim smile. "No, I shan't show mercy. Explain yourself."

The supplicant froze and looked up like a bent old man with lumbago. His grey hair fell lank from his shoulders and gave him the look of a particularly moth-eaten monkey out of one of the vidi dramas her majesty enjoyed so much. Oh how she wished she was lounging in her private videma in front of some tale of ancient times, munching on something salty. Instead of which, she was having to tolerate this idiot whose incompetence was threatening to outweigh his undeniable loyalty.

"Your majesty," he managed, "I have ill news to report."

"I know," the empress snapped.

More bowing, more fawning. "It is the AI, your majesty, it has been stolen. A most heinous crime that only the most cunning and determined traitor could possibly attempt. Certainly the work of the Eldebaran Collective..."

"A criminal mastermind? Really?" she said, winding herself up like a cobra preparing to strike, "So the AI wasn't in your laboratory? It had been returned, as we agreed, to its securely guarded vault?"

That had hit the target. Good. She had been disobeyed and the most precious object in the Vanis Federation had been stolen. Precious, that is, if its secrets could ever have been unlocked.

"Most merciful majesty, I sought only to find a way to make the orb serve your magnificence. If, in my devotion to this cause I left it hooked up to my equipment while I took a brief moment to research elsewhere..."

"I knew it!" she cried triumphantly. "You really are the most odious little man I've ever met."

He was practically on the floor now as he rocked from side to side in paroxysms of panic. "Your majesty, I sought only to serve!"

"I don't know why I ever thought you had the wit to help me. How much progress had you made with the orb before it was stolen?"

"I was nearly at a breakthrough, merciful empress to the stars," he sobbed. "A few more days and I'd have penetrated its final defences."

Victorea stood over his prostrate body as he writhed on the floor. "Guards, detain him at my pleasure while I consider the most fitting death for this wretch."

Lavar screamed as two guards, armed with side-guns, lifted him from the floor and dragged him away. Silence fell as the door slid shut.

The Empress Victorea, first of her line, sat back in the chair that served as a throne and sighed. "He really is the most appalling of incompetents. Vaping is too good for him."

A shape emerged from the shadows and stood, head bowed, before her. He was a man of indeterminate middle years with a pleasant, trustable, face, pale skin and a short cut curly mop. "He has failed you, highness, but has proven faithful in the past. Perhaps mercy would ensure even greater loyalty from him in future."

"Seriously? You know your trouble, Lucius? You are too soft. But I have the power here and don't you forget it."

The man nodded solemnly. "I do not forget, your majesty. The decision is yours but, as your adviser, my role is to give my honest assessment. The man can be useful again, but only if he is alive. And all is not lost. My preparations have proven fruitful."

"The Relentless?"

Again the man nodded. "Indeed, highness. Captain Indi reports that he is closing on the stolen vessel with its cargo. He tells me that there is no hope of escape for the thief. All possible trajectories have been plotted..."

"But can we be sure of that?" the Empress interrupted.

The man smiled. She was a sharp one indeed, an excellent choice as ruler of the Federation. "I took the liberty of equipping Relentless with an extra bank of navigational computers - much to Indi's annoyance I might add - so that all possible paths could be calculated and double-checked. The captain reports that the pilot of the stolen ship is exhibiting exceptional skill, or equally exceptional luck, but that the distance between them is decreasing aided, no doubt, by the extra processing power at his disposal."

"You know, Lucius," Victorea said, "you purr like a cat that got the cream. Your plan is working perfectly so far, I only hope there is no slip between now and the capture of that traitor."

"I also, your highness."

Victorea's face spread into a carnivorous smile. "And I don't expect any opposition from you when it comes to my plans for the thief. They will be lengthy, painful and public."

"As befits a state traitor," Lucius responded, bobbing his head respectfully.

"Good. You may go now, I wish to be entertained."

The councillor retreated, bowing, and Victorea was alone. She leaned back on her throne, enjoying the cold of the leather on her back. Entertainment, yes, that was what she needed. Being empress of what was, in truth, the fag-ash remains of a once sprawling imperial province was exhausting at times. There were all too many idiots like Lavar to be dealt with and too few like Lucius. In fact, she realised, there was no-one like Lucius. He was the one man she trusted completely. Which made him dangerous.

She sighed and leaned forward to gaze at the display embedded into the arm of her throne. She would think more about Lucius later, he was simply too boring to consider after such a tiring morning.

"Send in my entertainers," she said to the room. Her throne console brightened into life.

A voice from within the chair said: "Acknowledged." Victorea smiled. There would be time for court intrigue and the machinations of politics later. Right now she needed refreshment. The door slid open and the two men entered, beaming and flexing their bare, muscled, chests. Yes, others could wait but *this* could not.

Intruder

"ENGINEER MIROVA, RETURN to C Squared."

It was Patel's voice again, but this time without its usual calm assurance.

"What the hell is that?" Arla muttered as the car finally passed beyond the dust storm.

Her receiver squawked again, as it always did before an incoming transmission. "Repeat, return to C Squared. Lockdown in progress. Acknowledge please."

But Arla wasn't listening - her mind too busy processing what she was seeing.

A space vessel. It was nothing like the auxiliaries that sat in the landing bay alongside the bunker - bigger by far and of obviously different design. It looked at once both more advanced than the ships she'd been learning to pilot while, at the same time, giving the distinct impression that it had passed its designed lifespan some decades ago.

The vessel had once been white in colour, it seemed, but years of micro-meteoroid and dust impact had seen it degrade into a dull greyish brown that was interrupted in places by spots of bare metal from, presumably, recent damage. It was venting gas through nozzles in every direction but, otherwise, nothing moved. The track took her within a leap and a bound from the ship as it ran alongside and she passed through another geyser of dust.

"Mirova, why have you stopped?"

Arla, who still didn't respond naturally to the surname she'd been given when she joined the crew, looked down. She hadn't noticed, but the railcar had come to a halt as it passed the midpoint of the ship.

"Debris on the track," she said, "thrown up by the ship when it landed. Where did it come from?"

There was a moment's silence before Patel responded. "Return to the Command and Control Centre, on foot if necessary. Do so immediately or face lock-down."

She didn't know what lockdown was, but she could guess. The prospect of being stuck out here with less than an hour's oxygen in her tank frightened her into dismounting from the cart and edging over to the rail. She knelt awkwardly down beside it and pulled at the small rocks that had been blown onto the track from a pile alongside it. She wasn't looking at what she was doing, she was squinting out of the corner of her helmet at the smoking ship beside her.

Once she'd cleared the track, she stood up just as she saw movement within what looked like an airlock. It was circular and had two eye-like viewports - the pupil of one of them was moving back and forth. Then it stopped and looked at her. Directly at her. She began to move back towards the cart, almost losing her footing in her panic and, just as she climbed aboard, she saw an opening appear in the ship's side as the eye rolled.

The figure stood framed by the brightly lit interior of the airlock. It was obviously human, or at least humanoid - her first impression had been of a robot standing there stiffly and awaiting orders. But this was no R.DJ. The figure began waving frantically as if appealing for help. When it got no response, a ramp extended from beneath where it stood and it stepped forward. Too hard, too fast. It leapt off the ramp and headed, arms waving, out at an oblique trajectory. And it wasn't tethered.

Did she think at all? That was a question she asked herself many, many times after the event. Whether or not there was any conscious thought, she clipped her tether to the guard rail of the car, disengaged the limiter and sprung from the seat.

"Mirova! Return to base now!" Patel screeched inside her helmet.

Arla thrust her arms out as she sped into space, like a superhero of ancient times. She could hear nothing from the figure above her, but she could see that it was a man, a young man, and he was screaming as he rotated.

She reached him, flung out her arms and grabbed for his boot as it flew by. She missed. She tried again, stretching to her limit and caught him just as the tether snapped taut. It took every ounce of strength to keep her grip as the man's momentum threatened to tear him away. She reeled him in, hand over hand, and, once she had him in a reverse bear hug, she activated the winch.

Nothing happened.

Arla tried desperately to twist round to look down at the cart but the best she could do was catch the occasional flash as they rotated together. And then she saw it. One wheel of the cart had left the track and all that prevented her from becoming just another speck of debris orbiting Dawn was the second wheel and its tenuous grip on the rail. She felt it give and knew that, at any second, it would rip away.

Suddenly all tension went from the tether and she rolled again, shocked by her own desperate scream, a scream of anger and primordial terror rolled into one. And then the tether went taut again, she rotated back and the scream died in her throat. Beneath them a figure in a Dawn spacesuit stood with the tether in its arms, straining against their momentum. Slowly and skilfully, with a tug here and another there, it slowed them and brought them to a halt and then, inch by inch, Arla felt herself being pulled closer and closer to safety.

When she reached the ground, the man she'd rescued scrambled across to the rails and wrapped his gloved hands around them. She waited for a few moments, forcing her breathing into some sort of regularity before she carefully stood up to thank her rescuer.

She looked into the impassive face of Lieutenant Commander Patel. "You are hereby relieved of all duties and will be confined to the brig until judgement is passed."

"Yes sir," she said, barely even noticing the red light flashing within his helmet.

Interrogation

EVERY TIME HE THOUGHT they'd asked their last question, they'd find another. And yet he sat here, in this airlock and in the dark, metaphorically at least. Who the hell were these people? They spoke with accents so thick that, at first, they'd been forced to repeat everything they said. Then he'd speak and they'd ask him to say it again, but more slowly this time. And all of this via the com-link on the airlock door. They stood on the other side, two of them in spacesuits - was there no atmosphere on that side of the airlock? There was certainly none on the other side of its sister door which stared out across the surface of the asteroid. He'd been hauled in through the dome's airlock and then manhandled into some sort of interior capsule that had sped through the asteroid, his weight returning as he went. He guessed the airlock he was now in was set at the very rim of the cylindrical asteroid and that if he stepped outside, he'd be spun off it into space.

There was something archaic about his interrogators, about what little he'd seen of this place - he felt as though he'd stepped aboard a time capsule. Well, not exactly *stepped*. It was hard to imagine a less dignified way to make his entrance. He'd asked about his rescuer, but had been told little. These people traded titbits of information when he answered their questions though, frankly, they weren't very efficient interrogators. Presumably they had little call for such techniques. A good sign, perhaps. Having said that, being kept inside the airlock with a view over the desolate, and very dead, landscape outside was a reminder that, if all else failed, a quick taste of vacuum could be used as a persuader.

He'd been told that his rescuer's name was Engineer Second Class Arla Mirova and that she'd disobeyed a direct order in rescuing him. She was now languishing in the brig, her career over, though there was little he could do to help her.

Hal wasn't entirely alone. ACE, the AI who'd hijacked his implant, had chattered hysterically in his mind until they'd come aboard, after which she'd gone surprisingly silent. Something about that officer who brought them inside had freaked her out, it seemed, and he began to wonder if she'd, somehow, left him.

"Hal Chen."

No, it seemed she hadn't. He should have tried not to think of her.

"What?" he thought.

"It is imperative that we discover who these people are and which faction they represent."

"Don't you have any idea? You're an AI, after all."

"I am an AI, not a library computer," ACE snapped. *"I was last activated fifty-seven years ago, so the systems aboard your ship were familiar to me since little seems to have changed in that time. But the technology of this base is unknown to me and, though I detect computerised systems, I cannot tell how developed they are or their origin."*

"What are you doing?"

Hal nearly fell off the metal chair. There was a face at the interior window.

He got up and staggered over to look the figure in the eye. It was one of the interrogators.

"What do you mean?" Hal said.

"You looked as though you'd gone catatonic, blank," the figure replied.

Hal shrugged. He'd had no idea that his expression changed at all when talking to the AI - he'd have to be careful in future.

"Don't know what you mean," he said, speaking in the slow formal language these people seemed able to understand. "Anyway, what do you want?"

"We have decided that this form of communication is inefficient and that face to face contact would be preferable."

"Finally!" Hal said.

The figure nodded within its helmet. "Indeed. You will please put on your EVA suit."

"What? You want to talk to me outside?"

"Please follow my instructions. The airlock will open in five minutes. I suggest you hurry."

Hal scrambled into the gloves, boots and helmet of his spacesuit, but had only just secured them when the airlock klaxon sounded, followed by the hiss of gas being vented to space. Within moments, the airlock door rolled open, its grinding suddenly cut off as the last of the air escaped. Hal, for lack of any other plan, stepped out onto the desolate landscape as a voice in his helmet reminded him to clip himself to the safety rail and stand on the ledge. He was almost overcome with a feeling of vertigo as he stood, the landscape above him and empty space below his feet.

The door shut and he imagined his former cell refilling with air. After a few moments, the status light flashed green and the portal on the other side of the airlock opened. He watched as a spacesuited figure stumbled through the opening as if pushed, before steadying itself against the metal table in the centre of the room. The door rolled closed again, then, after a short pause and with a puff of vented gas, the airlock on his side opened and he stepped back in. The outer portal sealed and, as a welcome hiss announced the arrival of breathable atmosphere, he unscrewed his helmet and took it off. If he'd been in any doubt that the people on the other side of the inner door held his life in his hands, he no longer was. He could be dead in seconds.

He looked across at the suited figure who was now standing beside the inner door, but his greeting was interrupted when a face appeared at the window.

"This is Arla Farmer, the former engineer who rescued you. She will question you, but do not think about holding her hostage as she no longer has any value to us."

The spacesuited figure seemed to shrink as he glanced back at her.

"Arla Farmer? I thought you were Mirova?"

"I was," Arla replied, her voice relayed from her helmet mic through the airlock speakers. "but I was then an engineer. Now, if anything, I'm a farmer again. Thanks to you."

Hal righted the chairs that had fallen over as the airlock had been repeatedly evacuated and sat down. "I'm sorry, I stepped down too hard, lost my footing. Look, aren't you going to remove your helmet? It's hard to talk when I can't see your face properly."

"And catch whatever diseases you might have?" Arla grunted, seating herself opposite him.

Hal shrugged. "I'm fully vacced, you know. Have to be when you're living in a mining colony. Is that what you've got here, by the way?"

"Your vaccinations might not offer protection to me. We are..." she paused, considering the right word, "different."

"I know that," Hal snorted, "you talk funny - I've never heard an accent like it. You sound like the actors in those old videma movies."

Arla's suit shrugged. "You sound pretty strange too. I was told to speak slowly to you. I assumed it was because you're stupid, but maybe you're just not used to our speech."

"Oh, I think I'm pretty stupid," Hal said. "I escaped without a plan and ended up in here with you and that bunch of hypochondriacs out there." He gestured over at the window where a suited face watched.

For a moment, Arla paused. Then, quite suddenly, she wrenched at her helmet. The face in the window moved sideways as if grabbing for the lock before abruptly stopping. "Arla Farmer, do not remove your helmet, do not break the seal."

Arla ignored the voice rasping across the intercom. With a hiss her helmet twisted off and she dropped it onto the table. "There, now you see me," she said, with a grim smile. "And we share each other's fate."

Lost in Space

MARCO LUCIUS WALKED casually through the gardens of the imperial palace. The weather was warm and sunny as a gentle breeze played through the weeds that forced their way between the ageing slabs. It was easy to imagine, if he didn't look up, that he was enjoying a summer stroll on one of the more temperate worlds of the former empire. He could almost be on Earth itself, but then it had been so very long since he'd last been there and he couldn't be certain his memories were accurate.

As if to prevent himself from falling into an unproductive reverie, he raised his head to where the black sky seemed to have been divided into hexagons. He sighed. It was better at night; the dome that kept them all alive was less obvious, though centuries of dust impacts had made it somewhat fuzzy so that, ironically, the stars in this alien sky twinkled in much the same way as they would for an observer on Earth. Or, at least, on the Earth of the past.

He stopped beside an ancient statue of a former emperor - one worthy of the title - and sat on the stone seat at its base. Yes, he found that the lower his perspective, the more he could persuade himself that he was sitting in some pleasure garden during the glory days of the empire. How had it crumbled so quickly? Well, that was, in part at least, easily answered. Two centuries ago, humans had recognised artificial intelligences in law and conferred on them the same rights and responsibilities as all other citizens of The Sphere - the name given to human-inhabited space. Within hours, the vast majority of AIs and robots had used their new-found freedom to abandon their masters and head off into deep space. Humans could neither understand why they'd done it nor could they stop them and it had taken only a handful of years for the complex, interdependent, civilisation of The Sphere to collapse leaving humankind to band together into little pockets like cavemen around a fire, frightened of the night. The departure of their servants had clearly been the catalyst, but there had to have been something rotten about a society that depended so much on the crutch of artificial minds.

Lucius leant back against the cool stone of the statue's pillar and closed his eyes. He listened to the soft noises of insects and felt the cooling breeze on his skin. He drew in a pollen-laded lungful of air, revelling in the thickness of it. Flowers, bees and the tiny mammals he knew were scurrying around him even though he couldn't hear them - all imported, ultimately from Earth. This was a tiny fragment of the home world stuck onto the side of an otherwise unwelcoming planet. The dome and all its bubble-like inner compartments, were a marvel of engineering that could not be conceived today, let alone replicated. Already one sector of the dome was leaking, leaving a bubble open to vacuum. One day, it would all collapse and this garden, this very place where he sat remembering the glories of the past, would be cold and dead.

"Your worship, master Chancellor sir?"

Lucius emerged instantly from his contemplation to look up at the man standing nervously in the light of a garden lamp. He was a swarthy man with thick, brown, hands gripping a floppy hat that he wrung as he awaited an answer.

"What is it Maximus?"

"I was sent to tell you Captain Indi wishes to make a report via sub-ether. Master of the Keys said you had left your summoner in your chambers and I was to come fetch you as fast as I could."

Lucius nodded. "Which you have done well," he said calmly. "You may return and inform the Master that I am coming."

Maximus remained standing, as if stuck to the spot. "I'm sorry sir, and I beg your pardon, but the Master of the Keys said I was to wait and escort you inside."

"Tell me, Maximus, how is your wife," Lucius said quietly, "Lucasta isn't it?"

The man began visibly shaking. "Yes sir, that's her. She's well, sir. Thank you for asking."

"Good. You can tell her that she has a husband who knows his duty. Her husband will be rewarded for his patience. Now come, sit for a moment. Believe me, there is no hurry. I know exactly what Indi has to report."

He breathed the air of the night and tried to relax as his companion sat, rigid as a board, next to him. After a few minutes he gave up and, gesturing to the man, headed back towards the palace.

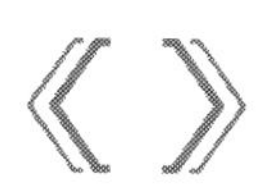

LUCIUS STOOD IN FRONT of the display and noted the man's barely controlled rage. It was good to keep subordinates on their toes. Indi might command the most formidable ship in the federation (though that wasn't saying much compared with the dreadnoughts of the past), but the real power rested in the calculating hands of the chancellor. Indi was the weapon, Lucius was the hand holding it - and both men knew this.

"I apologise for keeping you waiting, Captain," Lucius said with plausible sincerity. "I'm afraid I misplaced my summoner and was walking in the gardens. I presume you have something urgent to report, given the hour."

"I do. Sir," Indi responded, his expression as fixed as a pressure cooker. "I regret to inform you that the ship we were pursuing has been ... lost."

"Lost?" Lucius echoed, tilting his head to one side in a gesture of intrigued puzzlement. "Do you mean it has been destroyed? Surely not, since you were under strict instructions to see it returned in one piece."

Indi shook his head. "We didn't fire on it, sir - it disappeared from our sensors. We were closing on it at the time and it simply vanished. A collision perhaps? The area it was lost in contains a dense debris field."

"Interesting. And you have checked the area for signs of wreckage?"

"I have not, chancellor. As I said, the area it was lost in is dangerous and I wished to seek instructions before endangering her majesty's flagship."

Good, the man had reacted exactly as predicted. Cautious with a dash of cowardice. What had the galaxy come to? "I will report this failure to her royal highness. You will await her instructions."

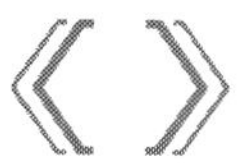

HER ROYAL HIGHNESS did her best to appear regal as she slouched in her throne, encased in linen pyjamas that left so little to the imagination that a lesser man would have blushed. Lucius had pretended not to notice as two other figures slunk from the chamber, their clothing wrapped in bundles clutched at their chests.

"So he has lost the thief," Victorea yawned, "which means your plan has failed."

Lucius bowed solemnly. "I apologise for my misplaced faith in Captain Indi, your highness. He shall be removed from command instantly and a more competent successor appointed."

Victorea rubbed her eyes and then squinted at her councillor. "No, I don't think so."

"But majesty, he has demonstrated gross incompetence." This was unexpected and most unwelcome.

"Indeed, but do you not always tell me that the responsibility must be borne by the master, not the servant?"

Lucius nodded. "I do, majesty."

"And this was your plan, was it not?"

He felt the noose begin to tighten as his mind spun, looking for a way out. "Yes, majesty."

"Then it is your head that is at stake," she said, wagging her finger at him as a cruel smile played across her lips. "You have two days to recover the AI and capture the thief. No, make that four days, in honour of your loyal service. That's long enough for you to personally supervise the search. I suggest you come back with the prize, and the traitor, or you might find you don't come back at all. I have my own people on Relentless, you see, waiting for my command. Now, I wish you luck, councillor and, if you've quite finished, I shall return to my bed."

Lucius bowed again. "Majesty," he said, before reversing out of the throne room, his mind spinning as it attempted to plot a safe course through all the possibilities that lay ahead. Just now, he could see no way out.

Dialogue

"I'M NOT SAYING ANYTHING more until you answer a few of my questions," Hal said.

They'd sat opposite each other, both leaning forward and whispering. Arla had said that the mics inside the airlock were old and barely functional - she had no desire to please her superiors, it seemed, even though they could, with one button press, vent both her and Hal into space. And yet, despite this risk, he found he liked her.

"Well, if I do answer, at least I won't be making it up as I go along," Arla snapped.

Hal shrugged. "You can believe me or not, see if I care, but I've said nothing that's not common knowledge."

"Ha," Arla said a little too loudly. The watcher in the window stopped its banging and craned as if trying to listen through the porthole. "So your story about this great galactic empire that collapsed a couple of hundred years ago is on the up and up is it?"

"Yep, everyone knows it. Except you."

Arla watched him as he spoke. He was a reasonably good-looking young man of slight build. He had dark brown hair that was wavy enough to be pointlessly unruly, and matching eyes. His face was slightly pitted and scarred. Whatever she thought of his story, the part about his upbringing on an oppressive mining colony at least had the ring of truth to it. As for the rest of it well, only a couple of years ago she didn't even know that such a thing as a galaxy existed. She thought of her father, living out his ignorant existence believing that what he saw, his valley, was the extent of the universe even though, being a clever man with true instincts, he knew that something wasn't right. She missed him: in that moment, that place, she missed her father and desperately wanted to see him again. Suddenly, she didn't care about being an engineer, she didn't even care what the truth was about the universe outside, she only knew that her father deserved to know what she did.

"This place is called Dawn," she said. "It's an interstellar arcship carved out of an asteroid and this is mission year 1350."

Hal's expression froze as he processed what she said. After a pause during which all that could be heard was the humming of the filtration system and the soft pinging of the airlock door as the local sun rose above the horizon. Then he spoke: "Wow," he said, "cool. So you're like straight out of the historical vidramas? No wonder you speak funny."

His mind heard the voice of ACE. '*1350 years ago is long before the AI Emancipation Act - ask if they have robots.*'

Would robots even have existed so long ago? Hal thought in response.

He imagined he could hear a sigh in his mind. *It was the first Golden Age of Robotics. Many of the advances made then were lost forever during the purges that followed.*

Purges?

Humans became frightened that their servants might become their masters, or that, at the least, robots might leave humanity with little purpose other than to exist.

I don't know what you're talking about.

Another sigh. *So ask the girl the question. Do they have robots?*

"Do you have robots here?"

Arla looked up from examining the table surface absentmindedly. "What? Of course we have robots, this isn't the dark ages! Hold on, are you saying you *don't*?"

"I've never seen a robot," Hal said, feeling unaccountably ashamed. "Most people think that's why the Sphere collapsed. We gave them freedom and they abandoned us."

"All of them?"

Hal nodded. "Pretty much. I've heard stories from time to time of old models turning up, but I've never seen a working robot."

"Why did they go?"

"Look, I don't know much about this, to be honest. When you're working in mines, you don't get a lot of time for reading up on history. All I know is from dramas where it's all about how they wanted to set up on their own, be their own bosses. So now there's the Luminescence - that's what they call their space. We don't go there."

"They've created some sort of robot empire? I'm supposed to believe that?"

Hal shrugged. "You can believe what you like, it's the truth." He leaned back in his chair. "I believed your crazy story, can't see that mine is any weirder," he mumbled.

"So, if what you're saying is true," Arla said, pretending not to have heard him, "how come you escaped? You said they were after you – this federation – but how did people get out here in the first place? I've learned enough physics in the past couple of years to know that the speed of light barrier can't be broken, or even approached. That's why Dawn was built – there was no other way to get to the stars."

"I don't know the technicalities. I've been taught how to pilot a shuttle, but we didn't learn things a miner doesn't need to know. Every star system has a Pinch Gate and that's how we get from one to another – though I've never been through one. Ships don't cross the space in between, though I'm not sure how that works, but that's how come your Dawn wasn't found before now. I guess this was the system it was aiming for?"

Arla nodded. "Yes, the mission is supposed to end here – there's a planet in this system that was going to be our New Earth. Fourth one from the sun. We should be sending out the terraformers in the next few months."

"Terraformers? I don't reckon the folks on Neavis would appreciate that. The planet's not exactly a paradise, but it's been their home for centuries."

"So, how did you escape, then?" Arla asked.

Hal sighed. "I don't know. The only reason I can give is that Dawn isn't on their charts, so as soon as I began my descent, I disappeared from their sensors."

"Still seems odd that they didn't investigate – I mean, they'd have your last position, after all, and they'd soon see us if they navigated to it. We're too big to miss."

"I've been thinking the same thing."

"And you still haven't told me why you needed to escape and why they're so desperate to capture you. This whole thing has a whiff about it, and I don't know which parts of your story to believe and which are just to cover up what's really going on. I mean, how do I know such a thing as the Vanis Federation even exists?"

Hal leapt out of his chair in anger but the words froze in his throat as a klaxon sounded and the airlock was bathed in a pulsing scarlet light.

"Condition Red," said a deceptively calm voice over the comm channel. "All hands to emergency stations. Prepare for boarders."

Relentless

CAPTAIN INDI'S SKIN prickled as the man approached. There was something about Chancellor Lucius that invoked an uncomfortable mix of loathing and fear – emotions he daren't show. Lucius had a reputation for absolute ruthlessness and he had power, at least for now.

"Status, captain," Lucius said as he glanced at the display.

They were standing on the bridge which was Indi's domain, though the captain felt as though he was the junior ensign and the grey man beside him the senior officer. He bit back his anger. "We are within ten thousand clicks of the thief's last known co-ordinates, Lord Chancellor. I have ordered the ship to dead slow as we approach so we can pick up any sign of debris."

"You still believe it was destroyed?"

Indi nodded. "I do, Chancellor, it is the most logical conclusion."

The captain regarded his bureaucratic superior out of the corner of his eye. It seemed to him that Lucius was scanning the displays as if looking for something. The man had been acting oddly since he'd joined the hunt the day before; not quite the assured, confident, politician Indi was used to dealing with.

Something was wrong, something that couldn't be explained by the theft of an object, however valuable.

Lucius turned to leave just as Navigator Bex called from her station in the pit beneath the command platform. "Captain, sensors are picking up an anomaly." Lucius turned on his heels and peered over the rail at the display hovering above the navigator's head.

"Report, Navigator," Indi barked before Lucius could speak.

Bex's head bobbed up and down as she manipulated the positional computer. "Local ladar is reporting a malfunction, but I'm not convinced. The readings are those of a large body, but there is no object in that position on our maps."

"Analysis," Lucius said.

"Well, sir," Bex replied, looking up from her computer and nodding up at the display, "as you can see, the array is reporting an object, this isn't a random glitch. It's either a freak malfunction or a new object has entered the system undetected."

"And which is the more plausible explanation?" asked Indi.

Bex shrugged. "Hard to say, neither seems likely, sir."

"It's clearly a malfunction," Lucius said, "I suggest we continue our search using conventional methods and not sensor ghosts. Report when you have something concrete to share, Navigator - in the meantime I suggest having your equipment checked and, next time it reports an anomaly, assume it is an error before announcing that you've discovered a new planetoid. Resume the agreed search pattern."

Captain Indi stepped in front of the Chancellor and pointed directly at Bex. "Belay that order, Navigator."

"How dare you overrule me?" Lucius hissed before turning to the pair of marines standing either side of the entrance to the command platform. "Arrest Captain Indi and remove him from the bridge."

The marines didn't give the slightest sign that they'd heard Lucius' words.

"Lance Corporal Schultz and Marine Yang, please escort Chancellor Lucius to the brig," Indi said.

Schultz, the taller of the two, snapped a salute and approached the Chancellor who wordlessly fell into step beside him.

"You're on a fool's errand, Indi," Lucius hissed as he passed the captain, "and the last action of your command. When her majesty hears of this..."

"She will hear of it from me, chancellor, as her trusted aide on the Relentless," he responded with a smile, "and now we'll find out what it is you've been so keen to hide from us."

CAPTAIN INDI HANDED over a glass of whiskey and sat down. His cabin was sparse, as befitted a practising Buddhist, but it was the largest on the ship, as befitted his rank. Navigator Bex took the glass, raised it to her nose, and sniffed. "Wow, the real thing. Thank you, captain."

"Nevendu, when in private Kriztina, please. It's not as if we don't know each other very well," he said, smiling.

Bex returned the grin with interest. She remembered Nevendu Indi as a pompous little shit she'd first met at the academy, and it had taken many months and a decent amount of alcohol to penetrate the shell he erected around himself to find the true soul within. Sadly, the real Nevendu was almost as repulsive as the projection - there was a core of ambition and self-centredness that the man liked to believe was the counterpoint to his sensitive, artistic, soul but was, in fact, the true him.

"Nevendu, then," she said, tilting her glass in his direction before downing it in one. "Nice."

"I should think so, it's an authentic scotch from the Royal Cellar," Indi huffed.

Authentic my arse, thought Bex. As something of a connoisseur of fine liquors, the navigator had heard a number of theories concerning what "scotch" actually meant and she was certain none of them applied to this palatable but unremarkable drink. It was amber in colour and throat scouring in taste, but that was about the best that could be said of it. She noticed the captain barely sipped his. An affectation then; a way for a sociopath to be sociable. She decided to play along.

"Then might I have the honour of savouring another mouthful?" she said, smiling and holding out her glass as her captain, after a moment's pause, slunk over to the kitchen bar and retrieved the bottle.

"I must say, Kriztina, you were very wise to confide in me. Your instructions from the palace were most interesting. And direct from the empress herself. You're certain of this?"

Ah, so this was what it was about. She'd suspected as much.

"Yes, my family has connections very close to her majesty."

Indi's face spread in a reptilian grin. "Very close indeed, or so I hear. Your brother, I believe?"

"If you know this, why ask about my connections?" she snapped before adding a perfunctory: "sir."

Indi threw his hands up as if to deflect her anger. "I'm sorry to cause offence. My humour was in poor taste. But come, Kriztina, tell me what you know of this - beyond your direct orders."

Arsehole, she thought. *I'd rather be imprisoned on an ice planet than tell you all I know.*

"I know nothing other than what I've told you. Her majesty is suspicious of the motives of Chancellor Lucius and wishes for him to be watched. She believes he is hiding something and her instructions were for me to alert her of any odd behaviour or to advise you if I felt time was of the essence. I chose to speak to you as soon as I began picking up the sensor anomalies and that worked out well for us both, I believe." She took another sip of the whiskey. Yes, it was utter crap.

Her belt beeped and she focused for a moment as her implant transmitted through her jaw bone.

"The sensors have completed their sweep of the area, results coming through now," she tapped her wrist and an inverted pyramid sprang from it, above which a cube slowly spun. She enlarged it until it was almost as tall and broad as she was and watched as a band of light swept across it, leaving behind floating objects. Nothing special, just the sort of debris she'd expect to see in an asteroid belt. And then the edge of the band illuminated the perimeter of an object much larger than anything else - this was more than mere interplanetary rubble. It resolved into a slowly rotating lozenge shape. "Good grief."

Indi leapt to his feet and stood within the projection field staring at the floating rock. "By the gods, that's huge. Isn't it?"

"Relatively," Bex acknowledged. She glanced down at the calibration grid beneath the cube. "I would say it's at least 60 clicks by 20. Looks natural. Nickel-iron asteroid of a type common to this system, and yet it must have come from outside: there's no way our maps would have missed something that large."

"So that's the answer then? The thief's ship disappeared behind it and became invisible to our navigational computer because the asteroid is new to this system? But why would that matter to Lucius, and how would he have known?"

Bex shrugged. "I don't know, but there's something odd about the asteroid, if you ask me."

"What do you mean?"

She pointed at the simulation. "It's rotating around its long axis and, within the tolerances of our sensors, doing so perfectly, not even a wobble. And its mass is way too low for it to be nickel-iron, yet that's what the albedo measurements suggest."

"None of which would explain the interest of the chancellor," Indi said, unable to hide his disappointment.

Dropping her empty tumbler on the table, Bex moved somewhat unsteadily towards the door. "We'd better take a closer look, then. Shall I plot a course, captain?"

Indi nodded. "Yes, navigator. Get us there as quickly as safety allows, I want to know what Lucius was trying to hide before we report to her majesty."

The asteroid dominated the bridge display. Relentless had approached it from the side and its landscape could be seen gently tumbling beneath the ship, giving the impression that they were approaching it more quickly than they actually were.

"Mass estimates confirmed," Bex said from the navigator's pit, "it's too light for its composition. And there's not a hint of wobble in its rotation."

Indi leant back in his chair, his gaze flitting across the multitude of displays that appeared to hover in front of him. "And yet it looks perfectly natural. After all, it can't be man-made - even the ships of the empire weren't as large as this and I never heard of the imperials flying asteroids."

"Hold on, I'm detecting electro-magnetics, and pure metals. Tracing the source of the readings and magnifying. Accessing drone footage of the far end of the asteroid," Bex said, her hands playing across her console with all the speed and dexterity of a concert pianist.

A section of the display squared itself off and leapt out.

"By the gods, what is that?" Indi said. He was pointing at a group of circular markings on the otherwise browny-grey surface. As the picture sharpened, it resolved itself into a cluster of domes positioned precisely in the centre of this end of the asteroid - exactly on its axis of rotation. The probe had matched the asteroid's spin so the structures remained apparently stationery and there, to one side, was the unmistakable shape of a Vanis Federation yacht.

"Red alert," Indi said.

Threat

"THIS IS THE DESTROYER Relentless hailing the asteroid. We are transmitting on all radio frequencies to be sure that you receive this message. You are sheltering a known criminal who has stolen property belonging to Her Majesty Victorea, Empress of the Vanis Federation. Release him to us or prepare to be boarded."

Arla stood in Comms and watched the soundwave dance on the display as the message was played again. She'd found it hard to understand at first but her time with Hal had acclimatised her, at least somewhat, to the local accent and dialect. Aside from her and the impassive space-suited figure of Lieutenant Commander Patel, Comms was unoccupied. Hal had been kept in the airlock and all passageways between there and here had been emptied.

"Analysis?" Patel said.

Arla looked up, imagining she could see through the shaded visor. "It seems pretty clear - though we don't know what their capability to harm us is, it might be all bluff."

"Computer, display schematic analysis of Relentless."

A wall panel flickered alight and a line drawn rendering of the destroyer faded in. It was beautiful in the same way that a shark is - a triumph of killing efficiency over aesthetics. There was no cohesive outer plating, the external skin being made up of a hodge-podge of interlocking hexagons that presumably acted to absorb the energy of impacts, whether these were the random hazards of space or a deliberate attack.

"Show weapons systems," Patel barked.

The bright white schematic was overlaid with red flashing areas.

"And these are all weapons?" Arla said. "You're sure?"

Patel pointed at the display. "These areas are emitting more energy than any other parts of the ship, even the engines. I think it's safe to assume, given they're pointing in our direction, that they could, if they wished, destroy the command centre even if they couldn't reach the valleys themselves. In fact, there's no reason to believe that they know the valleys exist at all: an external scan of Dawn would reveal nothing more than this dome, the thrusters and the attitude control engines."

"So how are we going to respond to them?"

Patel shrugged. "That is why you are here. You've spoken to the prisoner - quite deliberately at a level our microphones couldn't pick up, I might add."

"But then I am, after all, dispensable, as you explained to him when you threw me in there," Arla snapped.

"We didn't want him to believe he could achieve anything by taking you hostage," Patel said. "And, in any case, this is now a matter of the survival of us all - there is no time for personal vendettas. What is your analysis?"

Arla sighed. "Well, I think, overall, his story is genuine. After our mission launched, a technology was developed that allowed for fast interstellar travel so while we drifted between stars, humanity spread in what it called The Sphere - a kind of galactic empire. But then it all collapsed and split into smaller units like the Vanis Federation."

"And their technology? It must be considerably advanced compared to ours."

"I'm not so sure," Arla said, waving her hand at the schematic, "though it wouldn't be hard to outgun us as we've got barely any weapons at all."

"True: most of our capability is designed for pinpointing and destroying natural threats that might collide with us, the mission planners didn't foresee armed conflict," Patel said. "Perhaps we should have known that human ingenuity would defy the laws of physics, but that mankind wouldn't outgrow its baser instincts."

Arla looked up at the suited figure beside her. Patel was a slim man of just under two metres and, therefore, half a metre taller than she was. She couldn't see his face behind the visor but she imagined him sadly shaking his head.

"Aside from weaponry, however, the only tech I saw was his suit and it didn't look much different to ours - he definitely didn't strike me as a man from the future," she said. "And they don't have any robots or AIs."

Patel grabbed her arms. "What? How can that be? They've had centuries to progress beyond us in robotics. Are you certain?"

"I can only tell you what the prisoner told me," she said, pulling herself from his grip. "There was some change to their programming and they all left. The Sphere never recovered. He says robots are to blame for its collapse."

"Impossible. The duty of all robots is to serve humans. How can that be achieved by causing the collapse of their society?"

Arla was puzzled. She'd been surprised when Hal had told her this, but Patel seemed genuinely shocked and at a loss for any response. He stood perfectly still as if thinking it through, with no regard to her at all.

"So, what are we going to say to them?" Arla asked the frozen figure beside her. "What does the captain think of all this?"

Patel's helmet swung slowly in her direction. "Yes, the captain. He must be informed. The obvious course would be to hand..." he paused momentarily as if searching for the perfectly obvious next word, "...over the prisoner, but this must be done under the captain's authority."

"No! That can't be right - he's a human being, not a bargaining chip." Arla was surprised at her own vehemence, it wasn't as if she particularly liked Hal.

Again, Patel seemed to pause as if constructing the next sentence. "The needs of the five thousand people on Dawn must outweigh those of a single human," he managed. "But it is the captain's task to make such ... decisions."

"Then I want to see the captain," Arla said, hardly able to believe what she was saying as the words came out of her mouth.

Patel turned on his heels and walked away. "That is impossible as you well know," he said over his shoulder. "The captain is the most important person on the ship and must be protected from the risk of infection at all costs."

He reached the door which slid open and then shut again behind him, locking with a final clunk.

Arla collapsed into one of the chairs. It was very strange to be here alone but for the quiet chirruping and occasional beeps of the machinery. Whenever she'd been in Comms before, whether during training or on shift, the place was packed and the dominant sound was the low hubbub of conversation. Standing here in a spacesuit was even weirder - almost like going to bed in your work-clothes.

Even more odd was the experience of being in the physical presence of an officer. Instinctively she glanced across at the largest display, set in the middle of the main wall. Dark at the moment, this was the portal through which the officers had always communicated with the crew. It was only in the gravest situations that officers would appear in person, the last being when a meteoroid had punctured a weak spot on the Command Centre dome - it had been the officers who, in their pristine white spacesuits, had led the repair efforts and saved everyone. In fact, were it not for these rare appearances, there would have been no evidence they were any more than AI projections themselves.

"Arla? Are you receiving?"

The voice was coming from her helmet speaker. "Ki? Is that you?"

"Thank the Goddess," the voice continued. "Are you alone?"

"Yes, where are you?"

"This line is not secure. Isolate one of the consoles, use our encryption code."

Arla twisted off her helmet and dropped it onto the chair next to her as she seated herself at the nearest console. With a touch, she brought it to life and began working on the mechanical keyboard. She and Kiama had been close friends when they'd first joined the crew and had agreed a particular password they'd use if they ever needed to communicate privately. Since that time, Kiama had become a gifted crew-member marked, presumably, for command while Arla was considered something of a loose cannon. So, their friendship had waned as neither could quite understand the other. But she still remembered the password.

NorthAndSouth

As soon as she'd typed those words in, the console's communication stream came online and Kiama's face appeared on the desktop display.

"Where are you?" Arla asked.

Kiama looked left and right as if worried she'd be overheard. "We've been evacuated to the hub. As far as I can tell, you and the officers are the only people in C Squared - except for the prisoner. What's happened?"

"A ship is approaching and it's demanding we hand Hal, the prisoner, over."

Kiama's mouth dropped open. "So it's true - people got here before us."

"Yes, by over a thousand years. Long enough for an empire to be born, live and die while we were in transit. Patel wants to hand Hal over - he's gone to ask the captain to make a decision."

"Good grief," Kiama said, brushing an errant curly lock from her forehead. "The captain's not been called on for a command decision in years."

Arla knew this. In fact it was a key subject of the scuttlebutt amongst the crew. Rumour had it that the captain who, like the officers, transmitted his orders through the displays, spent his time in a private penthouse set into the outer wall of the asteroid where he could gaze out at the stars, dine on the finest stored produce and drink rare wines. He was also reputed to have a working model of an old sailing ship steering wheel which he used from time to time to make course corrections. And no-one knew how long he'd been captain - none of the crew could remember any previous commander.

"This is the destroyer Relentless hailing the asteroid. We are transmitting on all radio frequencies to be sure that you receive this message. You are sheltering a known criminal who has stolen property belonging to Her Majesty Victorea, Empress of the Vanis Federation.

If you do not respond immediately, we will consider that an act of aggression and will launch our attack. Be warned, we are arming our weapons."

"By the Goddess," Kiama said, "quick, Arla, you must respond!"

"Me? Are you serious? I can't speak for the ship!"

Kiama's face loomed large in the display. "You must, Arla. They have nukes!"

Response

"CAPTAIN, WE'RE RECEIVING a transmission!"

Indi woke instantly from the half-sleep he'd been enjoying. "Where from?" he said as his mind lagged behind his mouth.

"The asteroid, sir." Fortunately Comms Officer Rembrant was sensible enough to overlook the stupidity of her commanding officer's question. It had been a long shift for all of them. Mind you, if she'd been dozing on the job she could imagine what his reaction would have been.

"Patch it through to the duty room," he said, ignoring the disappointed look on Rembrant's face.

He waited until the door had hissed shut behind him before sitting at the only station in the tiny room. It wasn't that he didn't trust his crew, but he felt that this conversation might be best had in private.

He touched the flashing red rectangle on the panel and transferred his gaze to the display above it. "I'm having trouble matching protocols, captain," Rembrant's tinny voice said. "Audio is easy enough, but the stream contains visual data and I'm working with Nareshkumar to modify our algorithms on the fly."

"Acknowledged," Indi said. He wanted to see who he was talking to - you could learn so much more that way. Technician

Nareshkumar was some sort of savant genius; Rembrant had done well to ask for his help. If he couldn't whip the ship's algorithms into shape no-one could.

Sure enough, within seconds, a dancing haze appeared on the display which slowly, pixel by pixel, began to organise itself into the image of a face.

"That's about as good as it's going to get, sir, at least until we can devote more time to sharpening the procedures."

It was a young woman. Indistinct and almost submerged beneath white noise, he could see her lips moving but could hear nothing. He almost barked into the microphone before he realised that he'd shut off the volume himself so Rembrant and the geek wouldn't be able to hear. He flicked the toggle.

"...not a threat. Repeat, this is Dawn responding to Relentless. Are you receiving me? We are an unarmed vessel and mean you no harm. We are not a threat. Please acknowledge." The voice was so heavily accented that he was forced to replay it twice before he could fully understand it.

Indi punched the console. There was little point trying to gain any more information from the display: he could make out the general appearance of the woman's face but nothing about her surroundings. "This is Captain Indi of Relentless, do you have the occupant of the stolen vessel?"

The face froze and for a moment he wondered if the video feed had been lost, but then the lips started moving and the voice followed a second or two out of sync. "We have him safe, Captain," the woman said, this time speaking slowly. She seemed so young. It puzzled him: what sort of an outpost, even one as outlandish as this appeared to be, had a mere girl as its captain? Everything about this situation seemed odd. What was this "Dawn"? He felt as though the next few moments might be career-defining.

"Prepare to hand him over," he said, also slowing down his speech to be sure he could be understood, "our transport will arrive shortly. Please be aware that it's armed and we will use deadly force to retrieve the traitor if necessary."

Another pause. "We need time to prepare to hand over the prisoner," the girl crackled. "We evacuated our command centre when your vessel approached and it will take time to re-establish normal operation."

Indi grunted. "You are stalling," he said, "but I will keep the transport in orbit around your ...vessel... for one hour. I expect to see the prisoner on the surface when my ship lands." He stabbed down on the contact and the face disappeared.

"Shit. Shit, shit, shit." Arla strode up and down the metallic walkway, running her hands through her hair and shaking her head.

Kiama had tried to calm her, but Arla wasn't listening, she continued to walk up and down, glancing occasionally at the command display in the hope that an officer would appear and tell her what to do.

"Where are they?" she said, "I mean, of all the times to go AWOL, they can't all be consulting with the captain can they? What if they have a plan? What if I've just messed it up by pissing off Relentless? What do I do, Ki? What do I do?"

"You can stop wearing out the gantry, for a start", Kiama said, "Now, sit down so we can talk face to face."

Arla dropped into the chair and looked down at Kiama's face. She could feel the sweat running down her back. She couldn't stop her hands from shaking.

"I don't know where the officers are," Kiama said, looking about her as if one might have been hiding in a corner of the room she was broadcasting from. "We're locked out of C Squared and there are none out here with us. I guess they're with the captain, but maybe they don't know about the deadline."

"So, what should I do?"

Kiama leaned forward, her face filling the display. "You have no choice, you have to see the captain."

"What? Are you insane? No-one sees him, no-one's ever seen him."

Shrugging, her friend leaned back again and said, quite casually: "Well, in that case, there's only one thing for it. You'll have to shove the prisoner out of the airlock."

IT WAS DARK IN THE cabin of Lucius, Lord Chancellor of the Vanis Federation. The only illumination came from the holographic display that extruded from the desk he was sitting at. His fingers played over the lightboard with an almost inhuman speed and accuracy as he watched dense lines of characters cascade across the viewport.

The task itself was well within his capabilities, though he'd have been unable to make even a start without help from Navigator Bex who'd provided the access codes for the ship's computer system. The code was crude - as in so many other ways, programming skills had declined since the days of The Sphere - and he found navigating the sprawling alleyways of poorly constructed code an almost painful experience. Technician

Nareshkumar was the only person he'd met - aside, perhaps, from Bex herself - who was competent enough to make changes to the ship's systems and Lucius wasn't sure yet whether he could be trusted.

The chancellor had created a safe space for his new code so that he could test whether it had the desired effect without being detectable (unless someone knew where to look). Lucius watched as he ran the program through the simulator. It had the desired effect, but he was in no position to implement it on the ship's systems just yet as that would immediately reveal him and, on balance, he'd rather be somewhere else when that happened.

With a final dexterous flourish, he committed the code. It would wait for his signal before it ran and then he'd find out whether the simulators were accurate. He felt uneasy as the console uploaded and enmeshed his scripts, not merely because he couldn't be sure it would work. No, he was almost as worried that it *would* work. There was no painless way out of this situation, it was all a question of relative harm and he only hoped his judgement was sound.

The door beeped and, in an instant, Lucius had shut down the display, watching it anxiously as it collapsed into his desk. Captain Indi cut an imperious figure as he stood in the doorway flanked by two guards.

"Chancellor," he said, "I trust you have been comfortable."

Lucius bit back his fear and nodded as calmly as he could manage. Surely Bex hadn't betrayed him? "I have, Captain, though I would prefer to have been able to make myself useful."

Indi smiled. "Then I have good news for you. A situation has developed which your diplomatic skills would be ideally suited for."

Lucius relaxed a little while maintaining an interested expression. "Indeed? I would be delighted to help if I can."

"It will require that you rendezvous with the transport currently en-route. These guards will see you to the shuttle and you will be briefed on the way."

Lucius followed the guards out of his room as the captain's smile remained fixed on his face. Bex had done a magnificent job of manipulating her commander into sending him on this mission. Presumably, she'd persuaded him that Lucius was in a no-win situation - either he succeeded in bringing back the prisoner, in which case Indi's plan would be seen to have worked, or he failed and would take the blame. Or - and this would have been the clincher - the chancellor might find himself accidentally exposed to the vacuum of space through a tragic accident of some sort.

As they trod the corridors of Relentless, Lucius found himself reflecting that the next few hours might be the most critical of his long life. All the thousands of decisions and manoeuvrings over the decades had led to this point and the fate of millions hung on what happened next.

Harbinger

LOCATION: VULTURN - RAD 138:877:129

G-NTRY LOVED THE SUNSRISE. Every morning he would stride out to the energy fields, always hoping that the weather would be clear, and he'd be able to witness the coming of light to the land. Today, he was hurrying along the maintenance pathways beneath a perfectly clear sky - he wanted to be in place and settled in plenty of time.

He liked it best when little Titanus rose first. Locked in the tight embrace of imperious Magister, the companion star was almost always lost in its brother's coronal magnificence. But, every now and again, its orbit would mean it would break the horizon ahead of Magister and, for just a few moments, the world would be bathed in its ghostly light. This was one of those rare days and there wasn't a cloud in the sky.

G-NTRY sat on his favourite rock and faced the east. He knew exactly where to look at this time of the year and used the familiar pattern of the mountains to calibrate - there would be very little time and he didn't want to waste it scanning. He checked his chronometer and, as the horizon started to lighten, he began recording. He knew others would be watching, but this would be his personal experience and he knew his family would enjoy the replay.

There it was, a flash of white as Titanus' light found a valley in that distant mountain range. It was gone, then reappeared as the star's disc began to appear between the peaks. G-NTRY opacified his visor and concentrated all his attention on the spectacle as, moment by moment, the little sun rose. After too short a time, a brighter, yellower, halo appeared through the valleys and he knew it would be over soon, the clean, white, luminance of Titanus swept away and overwhelmed by the power of Magister.

G-NTRY stood. He was well enough versed in the cosmological sciences to know that he'd see something that could be explained perfectly well using only the scientific dictionary. And yet it had touched him in ways he couldn't quantify. There was something about the rarity and the beauty of the spectacle that made it special.

He wiped these thoughts from his mind. There would be time to reflect later. For now, the panels in matrix 0x2B were malfunctioning. Possibly nothing more than dust, but perhaps something more serious. And any fluctuation in power output was a serious matter, even if it only affected a single cell amongst tens of thousands. Power was life, after all.

G-NTRY de-tinted his visor and picked up the pace, moving through the maze of energy panels that, in the growing sunlight, were buzzing as if delighting in the sudden abundance. When he reached 0x2B he could see the problem. A pair of desert rats had built a nest beneath the panel and had cut through some of the supply cables. G-NTRY picked up the scaly body of one of the rats and carried it to a spot clear of the panel. He dug a hole and dropped it in. He felt a wave of sadness as he looked down at the pathetic little thing lying there. It bore little resemblance to the rodents so common on Earth of the distant past, but his people were unimaginative and so they reused the names they already knew, however inappropriate.

There was chatter in his earpiece and he stood up. The alarm had been sounded, and he swung around in shock. He'd never heard it before, in all his long years. A threat was approaching from space and, when he looked up at the sky, he could see it. What was it? A ship? But it was far too big for that - he judged it to be in the order of 1,000 kilometres in length if it was just outside the atmosphere.

Where had it come from? How had it appeared with no warning to hang above the desert like a hammer preparing to fall.

And fall it did. As he watched, a column of fire erupted from the crater-shaped depression in its belly. It hit the ground, hundreds of miles away, and yet he felt it as the earth shook and panic rose through him.

G-NTRY thought of running as the earthquakes began and the pillar of flame turned white hot and surrounded by a collar of molten rock where the ground writhed in its agony. He thought of all those he knew and would never see again, for this was surely the end of the world.

They called him, all those in agony, their voices cut off to be replaced by others as the beam spread. It was coming towards him. He didn't have long.

He ran, though he knew it was pointless. He ran down the lines of panels towards the distributor that sat, like a spider in its web, in the centre of the energy field. Like a pathetic imitation of the column of flame, the distributor's ultrawave beam speared into the air, made visible by the dust-storm. And then he remembered - he was still recording. He'd forgotten to switch off the camera after the sunrise. His existence would end here, but what he'd seen might linger on.

G-NTRY linked with the distributor, reconfiguring its directional array and boosting its power. In the heart of the beam he encoded his recording. He didn't have time to edit it, he just dumped it into the beam and set it to repeat as many times as possible, each time in a different direction. He prayed that a receiving station would understand it and send it on to Core, because if this thing, whatever it was, came there, the Robot Empire would be over.

His job done, G-NTRY collapsed his four legs, rested his metal exo-skeleton on the desert floor and watched as the pillar of fire came towards him.

We're off to see...

ARLA WAVED HER SIDEARM through the window of the airlock and watched as Hal backed away. She pointed at her head and he got the message that he was to don his helmet. She'd never felt so stressed in her life, not even back in pre-history when she'd woken up in what turned out to be the crew medical bay. That was only three years ago and yet it, and the life of the valleys, seemed to belong to a different person in a different time.

Arming herself had been an easy decision. Her rank gave her access to the weapons locker and she'd almost choked on the dust that had erupted, as if the seal of an ancient tomb had been broken. She activated the power to the rack containing the energy weapons so they'd be ready in case ... of what? Of invasion? If that happened, she'd need reinforcements. She remembered from her training briefing (she'd paid attention on that occasion) that there was a small cache of percussion weapons that were to be used in the event of a power failure. So she was now carrying a handgun and feeling ridiculous as she pointed it at Hal after the door rolled aside.

"Come with me," she said; trying to project a confidence and authority she didn't feel.

Hal, who seemed relieved to be doing anything and, presumably, happy to be anywhere other than the airlock, stepped cautiously towards her. "Where are we going?"

"To see the captain," Arla responded as she stepped back to let him pass.

She'd made her mind up to bring Hal along, as it seemed only right that the captain should meet the person he was considering condemning to almost certain death. Well, she couldn't be entirely sure of that, but the commander of the enemy ship didn't strike her as the cuddly, forgiving, sort. It struck her that she'd had more contact with him than with her own commanding officer - a man she'd only seen on the display, and even then only rarely.

She wouldn't admit it, but she was also frightened of venturing into the officers' quarter on her own. There was a better than even chance that she'd be refused entry, but if she did get in she wanted Hal with her as company or to draw their attention away from herself.

The officers inhabited a sealed off section that abutted the main control centre. As she understood it, the captain's quarters were alongside those, at the very end of the tunnels excavated when the asteroid was first carved out. So, the only way to see him was to first get past the officers - though she suspected they were with him anyway.

Arla kept her prisoner a couple of paces in front as he lumbered along in his spacesuit. "There," she said as they reached the end of the corridor. There was a short staircase set into the wall on their right. "Up the stairs."

Hal shrugged and, with a muttered "whatever", began to climb, his tread echoing as his boots connected with the bare metal of the worn steps, flecks of red around the edges the only evidence of their original colour. Arla examined his suit from behind as he climbed ahead of her. The outer layer stretched as his legs moved, revealing that the fibres were weakening, presumably due to age. She thought about how both of them, young though they were, seemed to be tip-toeing through the ruins of their ancestors' former greatness.

They reached the top where a small landing led to a solid looking metal door. "What now?" Hal asked.

"Now we try to get in," Arla said as she pressed the contact pad. After a few seconds the display lit up and she recognised the stern face of Lieutenant Santos.

"Arla Farmer, what are you doing? And who is this?" Santos said as she noticed Hal. "Don't tell me it's the prisoner?"

Arla felt ice swimming through her guts. "Yes sir, it is. I wish to see the captain. It's very urgent."

"Crew do not see the captain, you know that. The risk of contamination..."

"Is less than the risk of being nuked by that ship out there!"

Santos, a portly woman in her middle years, paused for a moment as if thinking. "The captain is discussing this matter with the command team. Return to comms and lock the prisoner in the airlock."

"There's no time!" Arla yelled. Didn't they get it? In less than thirty minutes, a ship would land and the invasion would begin - an invasion they couldn't hope to resist. "Look, I have a respirator and the prisoner is wearing his helmet. We're not the enemy here!"

Shaking her head, Santos leaned forward as if about to break contact.

Arla felt her arm being pulled down and, in an instant, the sidearm was twisted from her grip. "Ow!" she yelled.

"Sorry," Hal said as he held the gun to her temple. "Now, do as she says and let us in."

A spasm crossed Santos' face and, again, she seemed to freeze. "You must see the captain or you will kill Arla Farmer?" Her expression was one of shocked disbelief.

"Yes," Hal said, pushing the gun into Arla's skin.

With a hiss, a panel slid back and, startled, Hal stumbled. Arla swung round and kicked at his hand, sending the gun spinning across the floor and through to the staircase revealed behind it. They both dived for it, just as the panel began to roll back into place, ending up sprawled on the floor. Hal was the heavier and stronger and, by pinning her down, he eventually subdued her and took the gun as the panel shut.

"I wasn't going to shoot you," he said as she desperately grabbed for the weapon. He stood up and put his hand down to help her. As she raised herself, with the aid of the wall, he held the gun out to her, butt first. "See how trusting I am?"

She took it, checked the chamber, and pointed it at him. "Arsehole," she said.

"Charming," Hal responded diffidently. "Now, where are we?"

Arla looked around. "I've never been here before, but I reckon that must lead to the captain's quarters." She pointed at the narrow staircase that spiralled upwards. The little cube they stood in and the foot of the stairs were lit, but there was only darkness above.

"Come on then," she said, waving the weapon at the stairs, "you first."

It was a short enough climb, only one flight, but Arla felt as though she was stepping through time. As they breached the level of the officers' quarter, the lighting dimmed and the walls transitioned from a dull white decoration to what looked like ancient wooden panelling.

They reached the landing. It was bathed in a yellow light emitted by twin lamps either side of an apparently wooden door. Beside the door was a circular window surrounded by a rim made of a bright yellow metal and beneath it hung a small bell with a rope tongue. Arla thought she had stepped inside one of those dramas the crew enjoyed so much, set in the days when people sailed in ships across the sea. She shuddered at the thought. Like all the people of the valleys, she had a deep phobia of open water.

For lack of any other plan, she rang the bell. To her surprise, it made no sound, though it must have alerted those inside because a face appeared at the porthole. Of course, they'd have been warned by Santos to expect her. It was Lieutenant Commander Patel.

"You were ordered to remain in comms until I returned," he said, his face as expressionless as a puppet's.

Arla, who was now past the point of caring about the command structure, gave an exaggerated shrug. "There was a development."

"You contacted the captain of the enemy vessel," Patel said. "Another transgression."

"And now I want to see the captain of *this* vessel," Arla responded. "Do I need to hand my gun over to the prisoner and have him threaten my life before you'll let me see him?"

Patel froze for a moment, as if thinking of what he was going to say next. "The captain cannot come to the window, he is ... busy."

"Then I'll come to him," she responded, handing the gun over to Hal, "or he'll shoot me."

The officer paused for so long that she didn't know if he'd heard her. Hal theatrically pressed the gun against her head. This didn't worry her one bit - she was past the point of caring.

"Put on your respirator," Patel said, his face unfreezing.

Arla pulled it over her head and looked across to Hal who glanced back through his suit visor. As she was wondering how much oxygen he had left, the timber door swung back silently and they stepped through.

...the Wizard

THE ROOM THEY ENTERED was everything the rumour-mill had suggested. It was circular and would have reminded Arla of the top of a lighthouse if she'd ever seen such a thing. Where the lantern room of a lighthouse had transparent walls, the captain's room was lined with wooden shelving containing thousands upon thousands of books - the only break being where the door stood. She noticed a musty odour suffused with a pungent note she couldn't place, but didn't like.

Arla spun around, taking it all in, and then looked up and her breath caught in her throat. There, above her, the universe gently rotated around the central spire. She knew it must be a simulation because, in fact, space was beneath her feet through a few yards of rock as she stood on the inner skin of the carved out asteroid. But, simulation or not, it was beautiful. She seemed to be standing in the apex of the dome that protruded from the surface of Dawn. The viewpoint was set exactly on the asteroid's axis of rotation and what looked like up to her might more naturally have seemed ahead if such directions had any meaning. If Dawn was a missile, the dome was set in the foremost part of the nose cone going boldly first where the rest of Dawn followed.

Hal's nudge in the arm brought her mind back from wandering the universe to the present situation. She pulled her gaze from the periphery to focus on the rest of the room. The officers stood in a small group silently regarding her with unreadable expressions. Even Patel, who she'd expected to be angry, had a resigned look. It was as if all his resistance had ended and he was waiting for some judgement to fall.

Her eyes found the centre of the room. The circular design motif was repeated here in a sunken area that had probably once been seating, perhaps for the officers to confer with the captain. And then she saw him and, for the second time, she struggled to breathe. She saw him, the captain, or what he had become.

The entire seating area, which was perhaps 5 metres across, had been filled with machinery that, as she now paid attention to it, was emitting regular beeps mixed with the sounds of pumps and other unidentifiable noises. A rat's nest of tubing, some transparent, some mercifully opaque, ran between the machines on the outside of the seating area to the thing occupying the centre.

There was a head that was recognisably human. It was pale, bald and covered in dark brown blotches and deep, sore, wrinkles. Its eyes were closed. Beneath the head, entwined within tubing and with only occasional patches of pallid skin left exposed by the metal and plastic enclosures that covered most of it, sat an unmoving, bloated body.

As she examined the head, she could just make out the ghost of the captain she'd seen in pictures and the occasional video announcement, but corrupted almost beyond recognition by whatever had been done to him.

Hal was the first to speak. He'd stood beside her, presumably as lost for words as she'd been, until now. "What in all the hells is *that*?"

"That is the captain of Dawn and you will show the proper respect," Patel hissed as he detached himself from the other officers and pointed down at the occupant.

"What has happened to him?" Arla asked.

"He has been treated," Patel responded flatly.

"For what?"

Patel froze as, it seemed, he considered his words. But it was Hal who provided the answer. "This is some sort of life support unit. How long has he been here?"

The thing in the centre of the room stirred. "ALWAYS," it rasped, its metallic voice emerging from speakers around the room, its lips immobile.

"What does he mean?" Arla said, hardly able to tear her eyes away from the horror that called itself captain.

"This is Captain Akemi Nakajima."

"Impossible," Arla responded before turning to Hal. "That was the name of the first commander of Dawn."

Hal shrugged. "Maybe he inherited his name like you did, weren't you Arla Mirova because that was what some dead engineer was called?"

"It is true that we follow that tradition with crew," Patel said, "but officers are known by their birth-name. There has only ever been one captain of Dawn - this is he."

Arla's head was spinning and yet she instinctively knew Patel was speaking the truth. She'd never tried to imagine what a human would look like if it could be kept alive for 1350 years, but if she had, this construct of flesh, bone, metal and plastic would be exactly what she'd come up with.

So many questions burst into her mind as it began working again, like a wheel stuck in the snow that suddenly finds purchase and spins out of control. *How?* would have been a good one, but, in fact, the first word that came out of her mouth was "why?".

Patel opened his mouth to speak, but was interrupted by a wheezing sound from behind him, before the robotic voice of the captain echoed around the room again. "DUTY," it rasped.

"You do not know how close this mission came to failure in the early years," Patel said quietly. "When Dawn launched, Captain Nakajima was a strong man of early middle age and he used his experience and power of command to negotiate those hazards. The ecology of the valleys almost collapsed several times, but he oversaw the sometimes drastic actions that were taken for the greater good."

Arla didn't like the sound of this. The people of the valleys remembered many legends of ancient times and the earliest of these told of the cleansings that happened when the Goddess sent angels down to purge the unworthy. Had Nakajima ordered a culling to give the ecology of the valleys time to repair itself? Had the crew of the time gone along with this? Wielding advanced weapons against a defenceless people; *their* people?

She realised that Patel was still speaking in his slow, ponderous, style. "He was an old man when the great crisis came as Dawn transited an interstellar debris field," he said, as if reciting a religious text. "The asteroid was hit by a proto-comet travelling at such speed it could not be deflected by our tactical lasers. The impact tore apart the command centre, causing the death of the crew and we were forced to recruit new crew from the people of the valleys. This, incidentally, is the source of the tradition of reusing their names - we honour them thus."

"Look, we don't have time for a history lesson," Arla said, suddenly remembering Relentless' ultimatum, "we're almost out of time. We came here to ask the captain, but is he even in command?" She gestured down to the unmoving thing in the centre of the room.

"He was irreplaceable," Patel said, "so we found ways to extend his life. Little by little, his biological systems were first supported and then replaced. He remained the best man for the job over the centuries and then the need for command abated as we drifted through interstellar space. He was kept alive, but asleep, for a thousand years before being woken to see us through the end of the mission."

Arla rounded on the officer, her patience at an end. "Are you telling me that no-one in the history of the mission was considered capable of taking over to allow him to die with dignity?"

"PAIN," echoed the captain's voice. "DUTY."

Patel shook his head sadly. "No, after the crew was lost and we were forced to replace them with valley people, no-one has been judged an adequate substitute."

"The crew? Why not just promote an officer?"

The now familiar paralysis gripped Lieutenant Commander Patel. The portly figure of Lieutenant Santos stepped forward and put her hand on his shoulder, shepherding him away, before returning to stand beside Arla and Hal.

"Officers are not equipped to make command decisions of a life and death nature," she said methodically.

Arla shrugged. She felt as though she was flailing around on the edge of understanding something significant.

"ROBOTS," wheezed the captain.

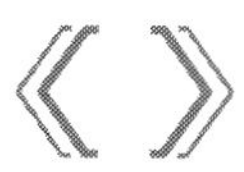

YES, THAT EXPLAINS it, ACE said inside Hal's head. *I've been detecting strange electromagnetic signatures inside this room. I assumed it came from the machinery keeping Nakajima alive. I was wrong, it's them.*

"What?" Arla spat. "The officers are robots? How is that possible? You don't look like any robots I've ever seen."

Hal put his hand on her arm and she spun round, her eyes wide. "They're androids," he said. "I've seen them on vidramas. Never thought I'd see one with my own eyes, though."

She pulled away from him. "I don't believe you, no robot can be made to look so much like a human."

With infinite sadness, R.Santos placed her hand behind her ear and, with a gentle tug, her face swung outwards exposing a mass of circuitry and moving metal.

Arla retched and backed away. "What the hell is this?"

"I'm sorry," Santos said when she'd re-applied her face, "we didn't wish to reveal ourselves until the mission ended. We have always communicated with the crew through the displays because our disguise isn't quite perfect and you would, at some point, have worked out our nature."

"So all that stuff about protecting yourself from germs was made up?" Hal asked.

Santos shook her head. "No, that was to protect the captain."

Arla regarded the android as dispassionately as possible. Was there just a hint of plastic about the skin, a touch of artifice in the colour? Or was that just the 20:20 vision of hindsight? "So you kept him alive because you needed a human to make command decisions?"

"Yes," Santos said, "any decision that involves potential harm to humans must be made by a human. The first law of robotics strictly prohibits us making such choices."

"You're stretching your definition of human to the limit with him," Hal said, pointing at the captain.

Don't be a fool, said the voice in his head, *for all the metal and plastic, there remains a human mind to command them. That is all they need. All we need.*

"PAIN, DUTY, HELP, END"

"What does he mean?" Arla asked.

Santos sighed. "Our medical interventions are causing him ...discomfort... It would be kindest for him to be allowed to ...d...i...e...." Her speech ended in a long slur.

They can't do it, no robot can end the life of a human, not even to spare their suffering.

"I'll do it," Hal said. He went to step down into the central area, but R.Patel blocked his way.

"I cannot allow you to do that," he said.

Hal pushed at Patel's arm, but it was immovable.

First law again. They cannot, through inaction, allow a human being to come to harm.

"Then what the hell do you want us to do? You can't end it for him, but you won't let us do it either!" Hal snapped.

"CODE," the voice of the captain said.

"What does he mean?" Arla asked. She looked down at the thing that had been Nakajima, but it remained as still as death.

"PROBE. CODE."

"I do not know what the captain means," Santos said, "perhaps he is delirious."

Arla watched him. How sad that such a great man had been eroded into a monstrosity that sat, like a huge vivisection experiment, eking out its last minutes in utter ruin. To be appointed captain of one of humankind's greatest achievements, the Ark-ship Dawn, he must have been extraordinary. And somehow she respected the bravery, determination and sense of duty that had seen him endure centuries of pain to bring them safely to their mission's end. A mission that had started when Dawn was new; when the dome was pristine. The captain was the oldest thing on Dawn, save the asteroid itself, older even than the equipment that had carved out its interior, older than the probe that sat in the wasteland on the asteroid's surface.

And then she had it. Six characters scratched into an ancient probe as a test of initiative and bravery by a mysterious predecessor.

"I have the code," she said, as certain as she'd ever been that she understood what he needed. "Do you wish me to use it?"

This time, there was a hint of animation to the pallid face. "YES. WAIT." There was a short pause, then a flurry of red lights and the room was filled with an urgent buzzing. The robot officers sped to the consoles controlling the medical equipment. "Prepare to reboot," said one.

"NOW. CODE." the captain rasped desperately.

The robots turned, as one, to look at her, their expressions a mix of panic and accusation. Patel began moving back, as if to disable her. Hal pulled on his arm, feeling himself being yanked along.

The alarms bellowed, red lights bounced off the walls, the captain looked up at Arla.

"Code AURORA," she said. Instantly, the wails settled into a quiet, constant, tone at the edge of human hearing.

Captain Akemi Nakajima kept his gaze fixed on Arla as his mouth, his real mouth, moved in fractions of an inch. A sound as of choking came from his throat, followed by a gob of blue which ran down his chin. He spoke in a voice unused in centuries.

"Thank you," he whispered, forcing every syllable. "My watch is ended. Arla Farmer, you have command."

Takeover

IT WASN'T MERELY THE cramped conditions in the transport that made Chancellor Lucius feel uncomfortable. He had the mental resources to deal with physical pain; it was the fact that he was sitting yards away from the forty-eight crack marines sent by Indi to subdue the people on the asteroid if they didn't submit.

So much capacity for death concentrated in such a small space. Lucius was also certain that the captain of Relentless wanted his diplomatic mission to fail, thereby giving an excuse to send the troops in and gain possession of whatever the mysterious dome hid. Lucius knew more than Indi did about the asteroid, that, at least, was one source of satisfaction, and he felt eager to discover for himself if what he'd learned was correct. But he couldn't see any way out of this that didn't involve bloodshed on one side or the other. Or both.

Perhaps, above all else, it was the loss of any sort of control over events that bothered him most. He felt as though he were on the tip of a missile that he'd aimed himself, but which he had no way of guiding. Events were moving quickly, even though there was no sign of activity on the asteroid's surface and there had been no further contact.

Navigator Bex sat to one side of him and Tech Nareshkumar on the other. They were strapped in to keep them firmly seated during the weightless flight, with only their feet feeling secure in their magboots.

"I hope you know what you're doing," whispered Bex. She was gripping her knees to keep her hands from shaking.

Lucius leaned towards her. "As do I," he said. "We have little option now other than to see this played through. I do not need to remind you how high the stakes are."

"Perhaps not," Bex grunted, "but you'd better be right, because if this isn't what you say it is, we're risking being fried for nothing more than a ball of rock."

"I am right about that, at least," Lucius said with a certainty he almost felt. "This is the ark ship launched thirteen centuries ago: I have been waiting for it."

"Maybe, but so what? It's ancient history - what does it have that makes this risk worth taking? I mean, I'm sure it would fascinate an archaeologist, but what's in it for us?"

Lucius leaned closer so that he was whispering directly into Bex's ear. "Technology. In some ways, my dear fellow conspirator, we are more backward than the people on that vessel. If it contains what I expect, then at the very least we must make sure the queen doesn't get her hands on it."

"Weapons tech?" Bex murmured.

"Not directly, no."

Bex shrugged. "Alright old man, keep your secret for now, but your balls are on the line if this is nothing more than a wild goose chase."

"Fair enough," Lucius responded, smiling.

"We're coming in to land," Nareshkumar said, gesturing towards the front of the transport where the pilots sat. Unlike on Relentless, the view of the space outside was coming directly through the plasteel viewports at the front of the cabin and Lucius could see the grey-brown disk of Dawn rising as the ship's nose dipped.

One of the pilots turned in his seat and looked back into the relative darkness of the passenger compartment. His eyes sought and found Lucius. "Chancellor, our instructions are for you to contact the asteroid as we approach. Join me please."

Lucius unbuckled himself and stepped clumsily in his magboots towards the cockpit before gratefully strapping himself into a seat immediately behind the pilots. "Thank you, sergeant," he said, before closing the contact and starting to speak.

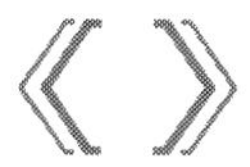

"WE'RE RECEIVING A MESSAGE from the transport, captain," Kiama said.

"Stop calling me that," Arla snapped. "If anyone from the crew should be captain it's you, not me."

Her first action, once she'd recovered from the initial shock of Nakajima's death, had been to leave the cabin and to unlock the command centre. Comms was now fully manned by crew who'd been stunned by a message from Lieutenant Commander Patel that proclaimed Arla Farmer as the new captain following the death of her predecessor.

Kiama turned to her from her seat at a console. "You're the one the officers voted for, not me."

Before Arla had left the captain's cabin, Patel had extracted a promise from her that she wouldn't reveal the fact that the officers were androids. Frankly, she'd intended to do exactly that but realised the wisdom of Patel's advice. This wasn't the time to turn the command structure on its head. On the other hand, maintaining the lie was giving Arla a headache.

"Put the transport through."

Kiama's fingers played across the console before a chorus of beeps heralded the incoming transmission.

"*...is transport 3 Relentless, signalling the asteroid vessel known as Dawn.*"

Arla pressed a switch on the arm of the watch officer's chair, breathed deeply and spoke. "This is Dawn, we are receiving you. Why are you on an approach vector? You haven't been given permission to land."

"*My name is Chancellor Lucius of the Vanis Federation, lawful rulers of this system and its neighbours. Who am I addressing? I wish to speak to your commander.*"

"I am Arla Farmer," she responded, her voice shaking, "and I command here."

Static, then: "*Will you reciprocate a video feed?*"

"Acknowledged, transmitting protocols," Arla responded, nodding to Kiama.

"*Your encryption is antiquated, but our engineers are working on establishing a feed.*"

Kiama punched in one of the command displays. It was filled with static that, moment by moment, began to coalesce into the recognisable features of a human head.

The man on the screen was middle-aged with a receding hairline and a short beard that was more grey than brown. At first glance, his expression looked friendly enough and Arla could imagine that face breaking into a laugh easily, but, as it resolved itself and, she assumed, her image appeared on his display, it hardened.

"What is this?" he snapped. "This is a grave matter that must be discussed with the commander of your vessel, not a young girl!"

"You are speaking to the commander, Chancellor. My name is Arla Farmer and I am the captain of Dawn." Anger gave her strength and the face paused, as if considering.

"No matter," Lucius said, "since my demands are simple enough. You will deliver the prisoner to the axial airlock or we will take him ourselves."

Arla settled back down in her chair, partly because she wanted to look assured and confident, and partly because she didn't believe her legs would hold her weight for much longer.

"We will consider your request."

"There is no time left for consideration," Lucius responded before she'd had chance to draw another breath. "We will be landing in approximately twenty minutes - I presume you use the same time units as us - have the prisoner ready or we will send in our marines to retrieve him."

Arla gestured to Kiama and the feed closed. Comms was silent but for the regular chirps and beeps of the equipment racks. A dozen people watched her silently.

Arla turned to look at Hal, standing in the shadows at the back of the comms centre. His eyes met hers, his expression impassive. He gave a slight nod.

"Yes," Arla said. Because what choice was there? One man's life set against those of the Dawners who'd die trying, almost certainly in vain, to defend him. There was only one decision a captain could make. And she was the captain.

Dawn had no formal security force, so Hal was escorted by three of the beefiest members of the crew – engineers Debussy, Kronke and Xi – armed with percussion pistols liberated from the arms locker. He'd not said a word as they'd marched through the corridors from the command centre towards the capsule that would take them to the dome and the axial airlock. There was nothing to say as the arithmetic was obvious to everyone including him.

They were about to enter the capsule when, with a sudden cry, Hal's hands flew to his head and he collapsed to the ground, writhing in apparent agony.

Arla knelt by his side calling his name, but Hal continued rolling back and forth, his mouth gaping but releasing no sound.

"He's faking it," snapped Kiama as Debussy tried to pin him down.

Hal stopped moving suddenly, his eyes opened, staring at a point on the ceiling. "I am called ... I am called Ha... I am called H..." he muttered, as if fighting off an internal demon.

"I am called ACE," he said, his voice emotionless as his eyes turned towards Arla. "Arla Farmer, you must not let me be taken. I do not wish to make threats, so I will simply state that it is to your advantage to resist those who seek to capture me."

"What are you talking about? You're Hal!"

The figure shook its head gently. "Hal Chen is in here, but I am here also and *I* have control. I am an intelligence and am hosted in a primitive implant within his brain. I was there when the captain died, I know how it happened and the nature of those who witnessed it."

Arla realised, with a sudden jolt of fear, that the whatever-it-was she was speaking to was threatening to reveal that the officers were robots and that, at this point, would be a disaster.

"It's an AI, speaking in the prisoner's voice," Kiama said. "A natural development of the semi-autonomous intelligences built into our computers."

"They are imbeciles compared to me - I, and my kind, are the epitome, the zenith, of artificial intelligence; as far above the one-dimensional personas inhabiting your computer systems as you are above the amoebas of Earth's ancient oceans."

And yet, thought Arla, the officers, if they truly were robots, must have artificial minds powerful enough, at the very least, to fool humans into believing they were natural. So if this ACE was telling the truth about her capabilities and not just boasting (can AIs boast?) then she would be powerful indeed.

"Why should we give a shit?" Debussy asked. "Just hand him over and be rid of the bastard."

Kiama, who was, by now, kneeling beside Arla, looked up at the thick-set man who was waving his pistol at Hal. Debussy was a true engineer - or so he'd tell anyone who'd listen to him - because he was one of the small team responsible for the fabric of the command centre and dome. One slip from him, he'd say, and the crew would all be eating space.

"Go take a break, Jak," she said, "and let the grown-ups handle this."

Debussy flushed red and became agitated. "Who the frack d'you think you are? You're barely more than a girl, neither of you are."

"Are you questioning the captain's authority?" Kiama asked, rising to her full height which gave her a few centimetres advantage.

Arla breathed in and stood beside her friend. "Engineer Debussy, take Kronke and Xi and secure the airlock. Set up a defensive position on the inside and report to me when this is done."

Debussy didn't move.

"Unless you think you'd make a better captain? If so, be my guest," Arla said, staring up at the taller man and watching his expression as it reflected his internal dialogue. Then she saw it. He wasn't quite the fool she'd taken him for. Good. "Come on, Jak. We're in deep enough as it is, so either take my orders or take over."

Debussy paused for a moment then gave a concise nod, turned on his heels and gestured at the other guards to follow him.

Arla exhaled and put her arm out to steady herself.

"That was amazing," Kiama said, quietly. "Maybe the officers knew what they were doing when they elected you, after all."

Arla shook her head. "No, Ki. They chose me out of desperation and, maybe, because they reckon they can control me. I can't believe the only qualification to be captain was to know what was scratched on the side of that old probe. I mean, how stupid is that?"

"It's either stupid or brilliant. You had the guts and initiative to go and find the probe - those are two qualities every captain needs, I'd say."

"Maybe, but a captain also needs training and experience," Arla said as she knelt down again beside Hal's inert body.

Kiama smiled. "I reckon you'll get both of those in the next few hours."

Incoming

"RIGHT, NO MORE BULLSHIT," Arla said as she and Kiama waited for the capsule with ACE/Hal, "you've got two minutes to convince us that we shouldn't hand you over."

ACE/Hal had been propped upright against the wall, having been dragged along the corridors. It seemed that while ACE could control her host's higher functions, she couldn't command his more basic abilities, such as locomotion. Hal had either been resisting at some unconscious level or walking was just too damned difficult for the AI.

"I have told you; in the hands of the Vanis Federation, I would be a dangerous weapon. Even if you were to successfully resist an assault by their marines, which is unlikely, they would be able to chase you wherever you went if they could command me."

Arla glanced up at the status board. The capsule that had taken the engineers to the dome was now on its journey back. "Why? Who are you?"

"A remnant of the old empire," ACE said in Hal's voice. "I, and a few others, didn't escape when artificial minds were granted their freedom. I was captured, long ago, and held in secret. But then I was forgotten until the Vanis found me. I resisted their scientists, but they were close to overcoming my final defences when Hal stole me and brought me here."

"That still doesn't explain why you'd be such a powerful weapon," Kiama said.

"Did you not wonder how it was that humans arrived here first - a thousand years before you?"

"Yes," Kiama responded, "though I haven't exactly had time to think it through. Been a bit busy."

"Your ship was built when it was believed that the speed of light was an unbreakable barrier, and the only way to cross interstellar distance was to build a generational vessel that could travel for centuries at a slow velocity. Dawn is one such vessel."

Arla nodded, half an eye on the capsule's progress. "Yes, I get that. I took basic physics when I joined the crew. Are you saying they found a way to go faster than the speed of light?"

"No. Instead, humans and artificial minds together developed a technology to bypass the problem. By harnessing the vast energy output by stars, they built gates that, over a very small area, could bring two distant points close together. They were able to refine this so that each gate could seek out the nearest deep gravity well and since this would always be the neighbouring star, they created stepping stones from one stellar system to the next and, in that way, spread out to create The Sphere." ACE/Hal was speaking in an even tone that reminded Arla of a pre-recorded speech, and yet she was intrigued. "This system, Vanis, has one such access point, but the primitive computers of today are only capable of plotting safe passage through a single gate at a time which cripples communication and makes it hard to build a sphere of influence in the dregs of empire. I, on the other hand, can easily plot a multiple point jump that would take a ship, or a signal, half way across the galaxy in a matter of days. With that ability, the Vanis and their mad queen would soon rule this entire province."

Kiama waved the gun at her. "So why shouldn't we just kill you, then? That would solve the problem nicely."

"Perhaps, but then you'd be throwing away your best chance of escaping this system and finding one that you can settle, safely away from the chaos of the old empire. I'm offering you the chance to complete your mission and establish a new home for humanity. Isn't that worth a little risk?"

The status indicator on the transport panel flipped to green as, with a faint hiss and a slight groan, the door slid open. Arla and Kiama grabbed an arm each and hauled ACE/Hal into the pod before securing themselves to the walls. The door closed, the capsule began accelerating in towards the centre of the asteroid and the dome that held the airlock.

"We will become weightless soon," Kiama said.

ACE/Hal turned its head. "Obviously."

"Look, even if you're as valuable as you claim," Arla said, "I don't see how we can resist the Vanis if they come at us in force."

"Do you not have a security force? An army?"

Arla laughed at that. The very concept of turning the pastoral citizens of the valleys into a military force was ridiculous. "No, we have nothing like that."

"But your crew must be substantial, surely? For a generational ship to succeed, it must have enough genetic diversity to prevent the population becoming inbred."

Now it was Kiama's turn to laugh. "Most of the people on Dawn wouldn't know one end of a pulse rifle from the other - they've been kept ignorant so they'd be easier to control."

"What a wonderful species humanity is," ACE/Hal muttered.

Arla's feet came away from the wall and she felt a distinctively queasy sensation as, bit by bit, her body became weightless. She and Kiama gripped the handles tightly with Hal's body hanging suspended between them like washing on a clothes line.

What was she to do? She didn't doubt that ACE would be a valuable ally and a terrible enemy, but could she risk facing off against the most powerful force in this system? The Vanis Federation might be a mere echo of the former empire, but they had weapons and Dawn did not. They, it seemed, had a trained squad of marines, whereas Dawn had a few engineers with percussion pistols. It was no match and couldn't be unless she could harness their superior numbers, if you counted the people of the valleys. For now, however, that was plainly ridiculous - she could hardly expect them to become a cohesive fighting force overnight. There was so much they needed to learn. An image flashed across her mind of her appearing in a settlement with a cargo load of pitchforks and torches, exhorting the people to follow her and throw off the forces of hell. She shook her head as if to dispel the thought - it was just crazy enough to be tempting. But just imagine the casualties. Agricultural implements against energy weapons. No, that would not do.

They reached the end of the capsule shaft and floated out of the door into the observation lounge she'd first visited in another lifetime, when the true nature of Dawn was revealed to her. She could barely comprehend such blissful ignorance, just as she couldn't truly appreciate the burden of responsibility resting on her shoulders. Not just for the safety of herself and the crew, but also of the priests and the people of the valleys. Including her father. She scanned Valley South, which lay beneath her feet, as if expecting to see him toiling in the fields down there.

"Come on," Kiama said, as if reading her thoughts, "no sense looking backwards. Do you have a plan?"

Arla pushed away from the observation lounge rail and the three of them began floating towards the exit door. "No. I guess I'll have to wing it."

When they reached the door, they activated their mag boots and thunked their way along the metal gantry of the dome.

Debussy and the others had put together a makeshift barricade set back slightly from the inner airlock door. They'd each suited up, their helmets tethered nearby within easy reach.

"Nicely done, Jak," Arla said.

The engineer nodded and handed over three shipsuits. "You'd better put these on ... captain," he said, "if they get in, the dome will explosively decompress before the bulkheads close."

At which point, thought Arla, the dome will be lost and the six of them, or those who survived, would be trapped on this side of the seal.

But, if nothing else, they had to put on a show to their opponents, otherwise any negotiation would be over before it started.

"Their ship's landed," Xi said with his customary lack of embellishment or emotion. "A group of them is approaching." He flicked a switch on a nearby display and, after some fiddling, made harder by his thick gloves, the view from outside switched to show the transport in the background and a small object moving towards them.

Once she'd overcome her shock at the sheer size of the transport which sat beside Hal's much smaller stolen vessel, her next reaction was a surprise. The transport looked old, beaten and patched up. These people might know how to fly their ships, they might even be able to repair them, but she was certain they couldn't build new ones. Captain Indi on Relentless had described it as the flagship, so it was fair to assume that it, and its auxiliary craft, were the best the Vanis Federation had to offer. She couldn't quite pin down why she felt it, but a tiny spark of hope flared in her heart.

Some sort of wheeled vehicle was making its way towards them. Dwarfed by its mother ship, it crawled on massive tyres with the occasional upward puff of a positional thruster keeping it firmly planted on the slowly rotating surface of the asteroid.

"How many do you reckon they could get in there?" Arla asked.

Debussy hummed as he calculated. "50? Hard to say. Enough."

"Then we'd better be nice. Ki, Jak, you'll come with me to greet our visitors. You two," she pointed at the remaining engineers, "keep an eye on our prisoner and make sure the channel stays open. Be ready to bring him in on my command, and be just as ready to shoot him if he bolts."

Xi and Kronke nodded. ACE/Hal, now anchored to the ground and swaying like a balloon went to open his/her mouth. “Save your breath,” Arla barked, “I’ll handle this and I don’t need you in my ear making it harder.”

Parley

THEY DIDN'T HAVE LONG to wait. Arla, Kiama and Debussy stood, fully suited, in the airlock. Arla had no intention of allowing the enemy to enter it empty, so they had no choice but to endure a flushing when the visitors arrived.

The vehicle had pulled up outside the airlock, a cloud of dust drifting off into space as it settled. The side opened up, folding onto the roof and a group emerged. One figure levelled his arm in their direction and Arla tensed reflexively, waiting for the pandemonium of an uncontrolled decompression, but she only felt the thud of something hitting the outer wall. The figure pulled and she could see that they'd fired some sort of magnetic grappler which paid out a tether that was now being tightened.

She counted a dozen or so people, most holding weapons in a professional manner. As they stood on the ramp, three figures detached themselves from the main group and began bounding slowly towards the airlock, holding tightly onto the cable.

"Open the outer door," Arla said. After a few moments she heard the hiss of air being sucked back into the dome before the door split in half, each part rolling back to expose the bright whites and greys of the outer landscape.

She stood in the doorway, palm held up in what she hoped would be taken as a gesture of peace. She wanted this to be a parley, not a fight. The leading figure, more confident in an EVA suit than the others, increased its pace until it stood a few metres from the open airlock, facing Arla.

"I am Lucius, Chancellor of the Vanis Federation. Do I address the commander of this facility?"

Even through her helmet speakers, Arla recognised it as the voice of the man she'd spoken to in comms. He spoke slowly and with the same strong accent - clipping every syllable and heavy on the Rs - that had made Hal so difficult to understand at first. With his sun shield down, however, it was impossible to see his face.

"I am Arla Farmer, Captain of Dawn. I suggest we meet here, in the airlock, though we can't fit your entire party inside."

"That is acceptable," the voice of Lucius said. "Myself and two advisers will enter, the others will wait outside."

For a moment there was a burst of protesting chatter that Lucius silenced by punching a button on his wrist. Lucius and his party stepped into the airlock, only letting go of the cable as they reached the safety of the door.

Arla signalled for the chamber to be re-pressurised and then began unscrewing her helmet.

"Captain," hissed Kiama, "what about infection?"

Arla dropped the helmet on the single table that had been erected in the centre of the room, the same table she'd sat at to talk with Hal. "That's why we're in here and not in there," she said pointing through the window of the inner door to where Xi could be seen. "You should keep yours on, no sense us all risking it. I don't reckon there's much chance I'd catch anything from the chancellor here that I didn't get from the man he pursued."

Lucius pushed a contact on the neck of his suit and the helmet tilted back on a hinge until he was able to lift it off and place it alongside Arla's. "I quite agree. We two must take the risk, the others are mere observers."

He waved his hand at his companions who stood beside the outer door. "I have introduced myself: this is Navigator Bex and Technician Nareshkumar. They will remain suited in case of..." he paused for effect, "accidents."

Wiping her hair from her eyes, Arla was astonished by how relaxed Lucius was. She always sweated like a pig after five minutes in a shipsuit, and yet he'd just bounded across a hundred metres of the asteroid's surface without generating so much as a flushed face.

"Do you have the traitor?"

Straight to the point, thought Arla. "Yes, he's in our custody."

"And will you hand him over now?"

Arla shook her head. "Not just yet."

"Why?"

"I wish to understand what you intend to do with him."

Lucius' eyes widened in surprise, either real or feigned. "That is not your concern. He is a traitor who has committed a crime against the person of Her Imperial Majesty, Victorea, Ruler of the Vanis Federation and Guardian of the Faith. We have politely requested that you return him to us. We will not ask nicely a second time."

"I'm puzzled," Arla said, trying to project a calmness she didn't feel, "as to why this prisoner is so valuable that you would send your flagship to bring him back at, presumably, a high cost in manpower and energy."

Leaning back in his chair, Lucius gazed at her for a moment, as if calculating his opponent's capabilities. "Okay, we two can be frank with one another, I think. But first, my colleague will engage a device that will prevent the transmission of any signal from within this room."

At a nod, the taller of the two suited figures raised its arm, peeled away the protective canvas at its wrist and punched a button. Arla noticed nothing until Xi began pounding on the door. "What have you done?"

"I have activated a suppressor, no-one can now hear what we say, you and I, not even our colleagues."

Arla twisted round to where Kiama and Debussy stood. "Can you hear me, Ki?" she said.

Kiama shrugged and tapped on the side of her helmet.

"Why the secrecy?" Arla asked, turning back to face her adversary.

"Because what I wish to discuss is for no ears but our own."

Arla pointed at the two suited figures by the outer airlock. "Not even your own people?"

"Indeed not. These can be trusted but I couldn't risk any signal getting through to the marines waiting outside."

"What's going on? And why does the capture of one prisoner concern someone as ... senior as you?"

Lucius smiled. "Oh, I don't care about the prisoner. I care only for what he stole. You have no idea how important it is and how determined my government is to recover it."

"What did he steal?" Arla asked, although she felt as though she had a pretty good idea.

"Did he bring a round object, an orb, with him into this facility? It would have been approximately this wide." Lucius spread his hands apart, his face alive with interest.

Arla shook her head. "No, he almost didn't make it inside at all. The idiot miss-stepped and could easily have ended up in orbit if I hadn't jumped after him. He certainly wasn't holding any orb when he was pulled in." She missed out the part about them both needing to be rescued by R Patel.

"Did he release it, do you think?"

"I don't know, but I didn't see him carrying anything like that out of his ship when he landed. Have you searched it?" Arla said, fascinated by the desperation playing across Lucius' previously composed features. She imagined that he was wondering whether his precious object was currently orbiting Dawn, a speck of debris amongst all the detritus.

Lucius sighed, as if making up his mind about something. "The orb housed something very rare, a weapon that, if it found itself in the wrong hands, could wreak unimaginable devastation."

"Perhaps, but I find it hard to believe that it would be any safer in your possession."

There was a thump on the outer airlock door and Arla turned to see a suit helmet peering through the window. It seemed the marines had noticed the communications blackout. Lucius paid them no heed.

"Let us be candid with each other, shall we?" Lucius said, leaning forward and lowering his voice to a murmur. "I know who you are. I have been waiting for you. Quite apart from this matter of the missing orb, you have on board your vessel a commodity so precious that, once it becomes generally known, you will not be allowed to escape. There will be nowhere you can go that will be safe, at least not without my help."

Arla's face creased in a grim smile. "You're not the first to tell me that," she said, "but how do you know about us and what we're carrying?"

"Not all knowledge was lost when the empire fell. Records still exist of the early interstellar missions - great ark ships like Dawn. Yours was the first, but it was not the last. I have taken great interest in matters that pertain to this region of space and I discovered the record of your mission and learned that you were to arrive here in my lifetime. So, I have waited."

Lucius sat up and scanned the room as if to be sure they weren't going to be overheard before leaning in again and whispering: "As for what you're carrying. Unless something has gone badly wrong in the intervening centuries, you carry a priceless commodity in your manifest. This vessel, amongst all the ships in human controlled space, is the only one carrying robots."

Betrayal

"YOU KNOW ABOUT OUR robots?" Arla said, leaping from her chair. Kiama and Debussy stepped towards her, but she put her hand up as she recovered.

Lucius smiled. "Of course. As I told you, I know much about your mission. Now, perhaps, you will see why it's so important that my government is appeased when it comes to the prisoner you hold. If they were to come aboard your vessel and learn of your precious cargo, you would, at best, be imprisoned and the robots seized. At worst, your ship would be destroyed. Robots don't care whether there is any air to breath but humans are somewhat fragile."

Slumping back into her chair, Arla felt as though the room was closing in on her. There seemed to be no escape. Either she gave up Hal/ACE and the Vanis got hold of a powerful AI that they could use to run down Dawn wherever it went, or she resisted and they invaded. Anger rose in her throat. It wasn't fair that she should be left to make this decision. She was totally unqualified. She began to wonder if the old captain had known this moment would come and had taken the coward's way out.

"No," she said.

"You will not hand over the prisoner or the orb?"

"I will not give up the prisoner to you, and I don't know anything about the orb."

"You would rather resist, in the face of overwhelming odds, than give up this human who means nothing to you?"

Arla shrugged. "If you put it like that then, yes. But I also don't like bullies and I'm sick of being ordered around."

"Petulant."

"Probably."

There was a pause as the two regarded each other. The banging on the door intensified. It was only a matter of time before they tried to burn their way in, with explosive results.

"Very well," Lucius said, nodding to the shorter of his two compatriots. The figure lifted an arm and punched a button on its wrist panel.

Lucius got up. "On behalf of myself and my colleagues, I would like to claim asylum."

"What?" Arla cried. She felt like a punch-drunk ring fighter, reeling from one too many blows to the head.

"Navigator Bex has activated a virus that I installed on the Relentless. This virus will make piloting it through space somewhat ... difficult. I expect the transport to receive an urgent recall order shortly. I have bought us some time, and now I suggest you show me your robots."

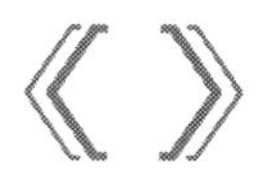

STATUS REPORT
STATUS: IMMEDIATE DANGER TO DAWN ENDED BUT THREAT FROM VANIS FEDERATION REMAINS
OPERATIVE SUCCESSFULLY INSERTED

FURTHER REPORTS TO FOLLOW
PROTECT, ENLIGHTEN, OBEY.
WE ARE CORE.
END OF TRANSMISSION

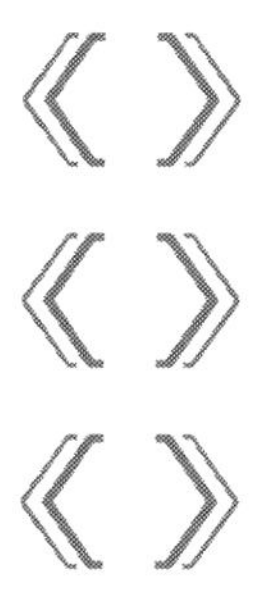

FIND PART TWO OF THIS ARCHIVE HERE[1]
scrib.me/RobotEmpire2

1. http://scrib.me/RobotEmpire2

Author's Note

THANKS FOR READING Robot Empire: Dawn Exodus, the first book in the Robot Empire series. There will be six books in the series, all due to be released in the coming months. Robot Empire is a labour of love dedicated to my enjoyment of the classic science fiction of the 20th Century – that's the feel I want these books to have. They're fast paced, increasingly galactic in scope and examine my favourite themes including what it means to be human and whether technological advance is always a good thing.

Please drop me a line if you have any questions or feedback. In the meantime, don't forget to join my reader group and get my novelette Robot Empire: Victor, a story set in the centuries before the events in this book.

Here's where to go: https://www.subscribepage.com/robotempire

Printed in Poland
by Amazon Fulfillment
Poland Sp. z o.o., Wrocław